HORROR IN THE WOODS

LEE MOUNTFORD

For my wife, Michelle, and my daughter, Ella.

FREE BOOKS

Sign up to my mailing list for free horror stories...

Want some free scary stories? Sign up to my mailing list and receive your free copy of *The Hobbes Hall Diaries* and *The Demon of Dunton Hall* (prequel to The Demonic) directly to your email address.

And that's just the start—as a *thank you* for your support, I plan on giving away as much free stuff to my readers as I can. To sign up just go to my website (www.leemountford.com) and get your free stories.

1

ASHLEY ACHED.

A dull pain radiated in her thighs, calves, and feet; pain that was growing stronger with every step. The air was cold and it bit at the exposed skin on her face. Over two hours of rain had drenched her, drenched them all, and the ground had become wet and soggy, making her feet sink into the muddy grass as she trudged through the wilderness. None of the group had been able to pick up a phone signal since yesterday, so they were completely cut off from the civilised world, and worse, she hadn't showered in over a day.

She worried she smelled like a dumpster.

Ashley was in good shape. Hours at the gym on the treadmill and weight machines ensured that, but even so this was still tough going. It was a different type of endurance.

Despite everything, she was happy and actually enjoying herself. Turns out Tim had been right; this trip so far had been fun.

She wasn't sure where they were exactly, only that it was the middle of nowhere, miles from any kind of civilisation.

However, that brought with it its own sense of peace and relaxation. Rolling green hills extended out beyond her in all directions, meeting a grey sky that stretched on forever. The smell of damp grass and mud assaulted her nose. For a city girl like her it was as foreign as being in a desert.

And yet she found herself loving it.

A big reason for that was the tall man before her who led the way, the one with the broad shoulders and nice smile, the one who had planned this trip for them and convinced them to leave behind the creature comforts of the city.

The four of them had fallen into a line: Tim out in front charting their course, Ashley in second, and her friend Kim just behind her, leaving Kim's boyfriend, Craig, bringing up the rear.

'How you guys doing back there?' Tim asked, barely out of breath.

'Not going to lie, Tim,' Kim said in response. 'My legs feel like they are on fire. I'm cold, I'm wet, I'm grumpy, and I stink. This is hell.'

Ashley smiled, relating to some of Kim's complaints. But only some. She heard Tim chuckle.

'Points taken, Kim,' he said. 'Just power through a little bit longer and we can set up camp and have a well-deserved rest.'

'And some well-deserved food,' Craig chimed in.

Ashley hadn't realised just how hungry she was, but after hearing Craig mention food her stomach began to grumble in anticipation.

'That would be something to look forward to,' Kim said, 'if we weren't eating rabbit food and rations.'

Another fair point. Ashley turned back to her friend, who flashed her a playful wink.

'Well,' Tim said, 'if you're hungry enough, even the simplest food can taste like a banquet.'

'I doubt it,' Kim said. 'But I would kill for a latte.'

'The closest we have is instant coffee,' Tim said.

'I'll take it.'

Even though Kim was complaining, and Ashley had no doubt she meant the things she said, she was at least saying them in a playful way. Ashley really wanted her closest friends to accept Tim and like him the way she did.

Well, maybe not exactly the way she did.

The whole point of this trip was to let Kim and Craig get to know Tim a little better and, hopefully, accept him as being good enough for Ashley. Kim was an amazing best friend, and she was fiercely loyal, but that loyalty could make her fiercely protective whenever anyone new was in the picture. When Ashley first told Kim about Tim, her friend had of course been happy and supportive, but Ashley knew there was a stream of judgmental questions ready to spring forth; and spring forth they soon did, in an attempt to ascertain his worthiness.

But for Ashley, the only question was whether she measured up for him.

She heard a click behind her and turned to see Kim sparking up a cigarette with her decorative gold lighter, the one that meant so much to her, which had been handed down from her mother. Given that smoking had directly contributed to her mother's death, Ashley found it odd that Kim kept up the habit, but she tried not to judge. Maybe it was some kind of connection to the past for her friend to hold on to.

'Might want to avoid doing that when we get into the woods,' Tim said without looking back.

'Excuse me?' Kim asked.

'Won't take much to start a fire.'

'It's soaking wet everywhere,' Kim said. 'I'm pretty sure nothing is going to burn.'

'It'll dry off quick enough,' Tim said. 'Just be careful.'

Kim's expression now stopped being playful, and she shot her friend a *who does he think he is* scowl. Kim hated being told what to do by people she knew, let alone a stranger, but Ashley knew why Tim was concerned.

How could he not be, given what had happened to him?

'Don't worry about me, Action Jackson,' Kim said, taking a drag and blowing the smoke up into the chilly air. 'I won't be starting any forest fires.'

Thankfully, Tim let it drop.

Ashley felt a pang of anxiety pop up in her gut. So far, everyone had gotten along, and last night Kim had even said Tim was slowly gaining her approval. This little exchange, however, had been the first signs of any disagreement, or animosity, and while it wasn't anything catastrophic, Ashley hoped it wasn't the start of a serious rift.

So on they walked, seemingly forever, until Tim stopped and pointed to the brow of a hill in the distance, one lined with a thick expanse of dark trees.

'There,' he said. 'We'll be cutting through those woods.'

Ashley wasn't sure what the difference was between a forest and just *woods*, but it seemed an inadequate description for the mass of trees that sprouted up from the hilltop. Even at this distance she could see that the green canopies at the top only stretched down so far, leaving weathered, brown spears bursting from the ground.

'And you know your way through there?' Kim asked.

'I do,' Tim said, not taking his eyes off the destination.

'Won't it be easier to just go around?' Craig asked.

'We could do that,' Tim said, 'but it's a beautiful hike through those woods. Trust me, you'll love it.'

'Looks ominous,' Craig said. 'Are the trees dying?'

Ashley looked to Kim and gave her a pleading look, hoping her friend would just go along with it. Kim took the hint.

'Looks nice. I think we can handle it,' she said. Ashley gave her a big, thankful smile.

Tim turned to look at Kim as well, with a smile of his own. 'That's the spirit, Kim' he said. 'A fighting attitude like that is perfect out here. Before long, you'll be like a natural at this stuff.'

She laughed. 'Not a natural, but I'll get the hang of it.'

They set off again, heading for the woods up in the distance.

It was a creepy-looking place, and Ashley knew she was the type to scare easily.

Timid like a mouse.

A few years ago, Kim had used that expression about her, and the name had annoyingly stuck, always on hand and ready to be used whenever her friends wanted to tease her.

Ashley the mouse.

There was no malice when her friends said it, but Ashley hated it. Still, she'd never told them to stop, which added further credence to the name. Worse yet, Tim had recently heard them use it and asked her about it, which led to a slightly awkward conversation.

Still, despite how ominous the woodland looked from here, she felt safe with Tim, so she dutifully followed him.

The group pressed on, dreadfully unaware that they were being watched.

2

He kept himself low, pressed into the dirty, wet ground.

They wouldn't see him. He was far too careful and too good at what he did. The forest was his environment; his home, not theirs. They were the intruders, and coming here was the last mistake they were ever going to make.

He bubbled with excitement, wanted to giggle, but even at this distance it could draw attention. So, he remained silent, exercising patience as he had been taught. It was hard, because all he wanted to do was to leap up from the dirt and dash towards them, screaming manically, just to see the look of shock, then horror, on their faces as he closed in on them. But that reaction, whilst exciting, did not justify possibly ruining everything. It would be nothing but a sweet hors d'oeuvre, and what he needed was a juicy main course. The pain, torture, and desecration he wanted to force on them was difficult to resist, but he had to, if only for a little longer.

It would come soon enough.

Things had to be done at the right time, for the good of the family. And the family were all growing impatient. The thing inside of them, that desire, that *need*, required release. And soon.

It had been a long time since their urges had been sated, and this primal drive was now fighting to get out, causing the family to turn on each other. That was fruitless, they all knew it, but you could only hold back instinct for so long before the animal took over.

Now they had fresh meat to feast on.

And the banquette would be tasty indeed.

He saw them trekking towards the woods, unaware of what awaited inside. Not just death, but torture and pain beyond their wildest, most vivid nightmares.

A smile formed on his cracked lips. The excitement made him feel giddy.

He squinted through the dirtied lenses of his binoculars. There were two women in the group, which pleased him. The one with long, dark hair and a confident stride looked East-Asian. It would be a thrill to watch that confidence crumble and melt into absolute fear. The other, the taller redhead, didn't carry herself with the same authority. Hers was the walk of a follower.

Those types of women were the most fun to play with. They gave themselves over instantly, with no notion of fighting back, putty to be moulded and abused, all in the hope that they would be spared.

Foolish.

And, most exciting of all, was a specific look they had, at a specific time. After being subjected to torment like they had never known they would still pray for mercy. It was important that he toy with them and dangle the carrot of freedom for a while. Make them believe they had a slight chance to live through it.

Then he would quickly and mercilessly quash all

notions of survival. It was then, when all hope had been stripped away, and they finally realised the inevitable was coming, that *that* look appeared in their eyes.

A look of terror so pure and so raw it never failed to get him off.

So lost in his thoughts was he that it took him a moment to realise there was a stirring in his groin, pressing painfully into the mud.

The group ahead was moving slowly, so there was time.

He lifted his body a little and slid a thin, three-fingered hand into his dirtied underpants.

3

IT HAD TAKEN ALMOST twenty minutes, but finally they stood at the boundary of the woods. Only a little while ago, the trees had been small outlines on a hilltop far away, and now they reared up to an impressive, dizzying height. The canopy of branches high above was so thick with leaves that it blocked out a lot of the sun's light, giving the bare trunks that punctured through the mossy floor a dark, ominous feel.

'Everyone ready?' Tim asked them theatrically.

Ashley saw that Craig looked to be feeling as apprehensive as she was. Even Kim's resolve seemed to falter, if only for a second.

'Fuck it,' she said, 'let's go.'

'Like I said,' Tim replied with a laugh, 'you're a natural at this.'

Ashley took a breath, which caught in her throat when she felt something on her hand. Tim had taken it in his own, engulfing it with his large paw. He gave it a squeeze and smiled at her.

Her apprehension began to dissolve and Tim led her

over the boundary, out of the open wilderness and into the woods.

It was a stupid notion, and obviously one born of a tired and slightly unnerved mind, but it felt like they had crossed over into something. She couldn't put her finger on it exactly, but it felt like a different kind of place.

But then they *had* just passed into another kind of place, hadn't they? They had stepped into a more enclosed forest area that had a completely different feel than the open hills they'd spent the past day hiking across.

That's all it was.

Twigs snapped under her boots and the moss that covered a lot of the ground was actually quite slippery underfoot. Ashley lost her footing more than once, but Tim was sturdy on his feet, effortlessly keeping his balance and allowing her to use him for support when needed. Kim and Craig moved up beside them, holding hands themselves. Ashley had a feeling it was more for support than any show of affection, something that she had seen less and less of between the two recently.

They had been together for so long Ashley had wondered if the spark had just gone. Was this it for them now? It led her to wonder if the same thing would happen with her and Tim over time, and if he would eventually grow bored of her and cut her loose? She hoped not; he seemed genuine, and God knows she wanted him to like her. Everything seemed to be going the right way, and he'd even opened up to her about something very personal from his past, something that broke her heart when he had told her. As a boy, Tim had escaped his family home when it had been set ablaze one night.

His parents and brother had not been so lucky.

So, when Kim had sparked up a cigarette earlier and

he'd told her to be careful, that wasn't just idle chastising; Tim was actually deathly afraid of fire.

And with good reason.

She took it as a good sign that he'd been comfortable enough around her to divulge that sort of personal information, painful as it must have been. Surely that meant he trusted her? And that, in turn, meant he liked her?

She hoped so, but that little, nagging voice that was a permanent resident in her head wasn't so sure.

Ashley tried to ignore her doubts and concentrate on the surroundings. Visually, the tall, tightly bunched trees were in stark contrast to the wide-open hills and fields they'd spent the previous day on. The air wasn't as fresh in here; it seemed dirtier somehow, more earthy, as if stained by the bark of the trees and the earth of the floor. It felt heavier, if that was possible, more musty. The sounds were different too; the chirping and chattering of wildlife, though sparse, echoed more in here, making the trees feel infinite. Like these woods were a place they would never get out of.

That wasn't true, of course, it was her mind running away with itself. Tim had promised there was a trail through here, and so it was. They found it shortly after crossing into the trees. And if there was a trail here, that meant people came through from time to time, meaning it wasn't totally removed from civilisation. It also meant that by following the trail, you couldn't really get lost.

As long as you stuck to it, of course.

'So will we make it through these woods before camp?' Craig asked. 'It's getting dark as it is.'

'We should,' Tim said, 'but there are clearings farther in where we can camp if we need to.'

Craig nodded, though he didn't appear entirely satisfied with the answer. 'And then tomorrow we'll hit town?'

'Yup, tomorrow we hit town,' Tim answered. 'There are some really nice pubs and bars there. Hell, there's even a good coffee shop so Kim can get her latte. Plenty to look forward to.'

'Sounds good to me,' Kim said. 'Though I may have to forgo that latte for a big glass of wine.'

'I like that idea,' Ashley agreed.

'Just imagine how sweet it will taste when you get there,' Tim said.

'I don't doubt it will,' Craig said, 'just seems a bit of a slog for a glass of wine. We could have gotten that back home.'

'But you have to see past the slog,' Ashley said, feeling the need to back Tim up. 'It's really nice out here and totally different to what we're used to. Let's be honest, it'll do us all good to get out of the city for a few days, to see this side of the world.'

Tim gently squeezed her hand.

'Fair point,' Kim said. 'Craig, stop complaining, I think we should all try our best to enjoy this.'

'I guess,' Craig said. 'It's just so creepy out here.'

Tim gave a conspiratorial wink to Ashley. 'It would be even more creepy if you knew the stories.'

Craig stopped in his tracks. 'What stories?'

'Relax, they aren't real, just urban legends about this place. These woods, specifically.'

'Oh great, this place is haunted, isn't it?' Craig asked, and the others stopped too.

'Not exactly,' Tim replied, 'but if you believe the stories, there are things out here. Things waiting to prey on hikers and people who wander in uninvited.'

Ashley caught eyes with Kim and give her a sly smile, letting her in on the joke. Kim nodded her understanding.

'Things? Can you be more specific?' Craig asked him.

'Do you want me to be?'

Craig sighed. 'I'm not sure, to be honest.'

'Don't stress about it, Craig,' Kim said. 'It's not like you believe in anything like that.'

'I don't, but—'

'Exactly,' Tim cut in. 'Like I said, it's just an urban legend. They exist everywhere. I'm pretty sure the Webb family isn't real. At best, they're a twist on a family that maybe lived here years ago.'

'The Webb family?'

'Yeah, a family that is supposed to live out here in the woods. Not nice people.'

Ashley was struggling to keep from bursting into laughter, though she did feel bad for Craig. She could see the story, as outlandish and bare bones as it was, was beginning to unsettle him a little. The whole thing was made worse by the fact that Kim was ever-so-stealthily making her way behind Craig as he was engrossed by the wild yarn Tim was spinning.

'Let me guess,' Craig said, 'a family of killers?'

'Bingo,' Tim said, poker-faced. 'Not just killers, though, they are supposed to be twisted, demented deviants. They don't just kill, they torture. And they eat people while they're still alive.'

'Ah, cannibals as well, then. How very cliché.'

'Yeah,' Tim said, nodding in agreement, 'most legends are. They say that this family has a specific reason for doing what they do. Well, other than enjoyment, that is.'

'And what reason is that?'

Kim was directly behind Craig now and Ashley was amazed he hadn't seen her. She had to bite her bottom lip to keep the laughter from erupting out of her.

'Story goes that there is something else in these woods, too. Something kind of old, ancient evil. Something that has found its way up from the-devil-knows-where. Maybe hell itself. This thing is, apparently, what the Webb's serve. And in return, they are granted special privileges.'

'Such as?'

'Can't say for sure, but it sure fuels their hunger for human meat. It's why they kill whoever comes through here. Hell, they could be out there somewhere right now, watching us.'

Kim chose that moment to throw her arms around Craig and scream in his ear. 'Craiiiiig!'

Craig nearly jumped out of his skin and threw Kim off him. He even let out an audible scream, something Ashley knew would only embarrass him further when he had regained his composure.

'Get off,' he said, his face going beet red. 'You bunch of dicks.'

The rest of the group were almost doubled over in laughter, especially Kim, clearly proud of her role in the prank.

'Oh Craig,' she said through teary eyes, 'you jumped like a scalded cat.'

'It wasn't funny,' he said, trying to calm down. His ego had obviously taken a knock. Ashley did feel bad for him, but that wasn't enough to stop her laughter.

'Sorry, Craig,' Tim said. 'It was just a joke.'

'Well ha-ha. Very funny. The story was stupid anyway, why would anyone believe it was true?'

'You seemed to believe it when you squealed like a girl,' Kim said, digging him in the ribs with her fingers. He batted her hand away.

'Oh, it is a true story,' Tim said. 'Well, maybe I misspoke, it's a story that people around here have actually told over the years.'

'Well, it's still stupid,'

'I agree,' Tim answered.

'Let's just keep moving,' Craig decided, walking off ahead in a sulk and leaving the other three behind. 'The sooner we're out of this place, the better.'

Kim rolled her eyes and mouthed the word, *baby*, before going after him. She fell in line with him and Ashley heard their muted talking. She and Tim set off behind, giving them a little room.

'I didn't go too far, did I?' Tim asked. 'I was only trying to lighten the mood.'

'Don't worry about it,' Ashley said. 'He'll get over it before long. He's just not the best at handling being the butt of a joke.'

'I can understand that,' Tim said. 'I'll apologise later.'

'You don't have to.'

'I know, but I will. No need to give anyone a reason not to like me. They're your friends, so I'm trying to get them onboard.'

'They will like you,' Ashley said. 'Just be yourself and they can't *not* fall in love with you.'

'Is that right?'

'I did,' Ashley said. As soon as the words had left her lips, her body seized up.

Shit, shit, shit!

Ashley realised she'd just told Tim she loved him. They'd never discussed it before, and she had no idea she felt that strongly, but after saying it, it didn't feel like she had misspoken. The problem was that it was out there now, hanging over them like a bad smell. Ashley felt a knot tighten in her stomach. How would he react?

Would he tense up, pull away, murmur how he thinks she's *nice*? She looked away, wanting the ground to swallow her up, but felt his hand cup her chin and pull her gaze back to him.

He was smiling.

'You beat me to the punch,' he said.

'Really?'

'Yeah, I was planning on telling you tonight, maybe snuggled round a fire. Something romantic.'

'I... I don't know what to say.'

He laughed. 'Well, you can apologise for ruining my best-laid plans.'

He then pulled her towards him and kissed her, with passion. The knot in her stomach freed itself, and a burst of adrenaline rippled through her. She kissed him back and ran her hand through his hair. She pressed her body against his, overcome in the moment, and she felt him growing excited.

'Well then,' she said, whispering in his ear, 'I think we can still make tonight special. But you're going to have to control yourself for a little while longer.'

'I can try,' he grinned. 'But you don't make it easy.'

She shrugged and skipped off ahead, trying to play the tease. Not a role that came naturally. 'You'd find me boring if I did that.'

Ashley felt elated.

It was the first time she'd ever told anybody she loved them. And worse, it wasn't planned, it had just slipped out with barely any thought. Those few moments where she was twisting in the wind felt like an eternity, but hearing him say that he felt the same way made it worth it. She felt him catch up to her and take her hand again, his goofy grin as big as hers.

The moment was then ruined by Kim.

'What the fuck is that?'

Just up ahead, Kim and Craig had stopped dead in their tracks, their bodies tense.

'What is it?' Tim asked.

Kim didn't answer directly. 'Is he...?'

'Can't be,' Craig said, his voice quiet. Scared.

'What?' Ashley asked as she and Tim jogged over.

Ashley shrieked when she saw what they were looking at. A cold feeling crawled its way up her spine.

A man lay on the ground beyond them, tied and bound.

He was, without a doubt, quite dead.

And he had also been stripped of his face.

4

THAT WAS UNEXPECTED.

It seemed the group he was following had stumbled upon a little surprise. One that lay motionless and bound on the floor. Skin torn from the face.

That must have been painful!

But the development concerned him.

It could ruin everything.

He had been following the group undetected for a while now, but out in the wilderness he had to keep a good distance. Now, under the cover and darkness of the trees, he felt even more sure of himself, with more places to hide, and was able to stay closer to them.

He was the wolf and they were little, vulnerable sheep, ripe for a messy slaughter.

But the sight the group were now looking at in the small clearing certainly mixed things up a little. Though maybe not in a bad way. It would certainly raise their fears and tensions, which was good. It got them scared earlier, and it would make playing with them that much more fun. He just hoped it wouldn't make them turn back on themselves, because then the trap would turn into a hunt.

Not that hunting them down didn't have its appeal. Chasing them as they ran for their lives, squealing like pigs. But it's not how things were supposed to go. There was more risk that way, if only a little.

He watched as one of them began taking tentative steps towards what they had found. He kept his eyes on the redhead, who didn't move at all, and focused on her nicely rounded rear. He debated pleasing himself again; certainly the mood was rising, he could feel the stirring again. But he knew he couldn't, things could change quickly given the current turn of events and he needed to be ready.

If he failed and the family were denied their food, Father and Mother would hold him accountable and there would be hell to pay.

He did not plan on letting them down.

5

Ashley couldn't quite believe what she was seeing.

Tim and Craig slowly approached the body, but Ashley didn't want to move; she wanted to keep as far away from it as possible. When Kim began to walk to the body as well, Ashley was left with no choice but to follow. She didn't want to look—she had no desire to investigate such a morbid scene—but she didn't want to be removed from the group, even by a few feet. Her legs wobbled as she took tentative steps. The closer she got, the clearer the horrific sight became.

At first, at a distance, the man's face just seemed like a red smudge, like it had been covered in crimson paint, but the closer she got, the more detail she saw, and the more nauseous she felt.

The face had been torn off completely and Ashley could make out lumps of flesh and tendons still attached to the grinning skull beneath.

'Oh God,' Kim said.

The group stopped as one about ten yards from him,

sharing a seemingly telepathic agreement not to get any closer.

'What happened to him?' Ashley asked.

She looked to Tim, who just shrugged. 'I have no idea.'

'His face...' Ashley went on, but felt herself trail off.

'What could do something like that?' Craig asked. 'Maybe an animal or something?'

Again, Tim shrugged. 'Could be, I suppose. If he was already dead. Though I'm not sure what kind of animals around here would have done that. A hungry fox, maybe?'

'I don't think that's what it was,' Ashley said, pointing. 'Look at his hands.'

They all saw what she was seeing. The man's hands were bound together in front of him with what looked like thin wire wrapped tightly around his wrists, cutting into the skin.

'Fuck,' Kim said.

'Someone killed him?' Craig asked.

'I don't think so,' Tim said.

'So he just lay down, tied himself up, and let the animals eat his face?' Kim said, with no small amount of sarcasm.

Ashley looked around, feeling an uneasy sensation crawl over her. Then she saw it, a few yards from them, hanging from a branch, swaying in the gentle breeze like a rag.

She began to scream, horrified at the sight. Her instinct was to huddle down to the floor and cover her eyes.

'What is it?' Kim asked, panicked. She crouched next to Ashley and put an arm around her shoulders. 'What's wrong?'

Once again, Ashley pointed, and the others followed the gesture.

Hanging from a nearby branch, jagged and bloody—like a macabre mask—was the flap of skin that had been torn from the man.

KIM WANTED TO SCREAM, just like Ashley already was.

It was there, lodged in her dry throat somewhere, but she refused to let it out. Instead, she looked on, horrified, at what was hanging in front of them. It was a surreal, terrifying sight.

The face before them obviously belonged to the poor man who lay dead only feet away from them, but Kim's mind ran to more urgent thoughts.

It was clear that someone had murdered him.

Whoever it was, they had killed the man for reasons Kim didn't know—would probably never know—and that was bad enough, but they'd also saw fit to leave his face on display like some kind of warning.

Or taunt.

So, the question was, who was it meant to taunt?

The smell of blood was strong and fresh, so Kim was acutely aware that whoever had killed the man was probably still out there in the woods somewhere.

Still hugging her screaming friend, Kim put her hands against Ashley's cheeks and twisted her face to meet her own, away from that horrible sight.

'Ashley, honey,' she said, in the most soothing tones she could muster. 'You need to stop yelling.'

'But look at it,' Ashley said, her breathing heavy and erratic.

'I know, I know. But we need to try to be calm, hun. We need to be quiet.'

Kim saw the realisation dawn over her friend. 'Because, they could still be out here?' she said.

Kim nodded. Ashley shut her eyes tight and began to

cry, but it was a quiet sob, one pushed down within. Kim pulled Ashley in and hugged her.

'It's going to be okay,' she whispered.

'Tim,' she heard Craig say, his voice unsteady. 'What the fuck is this?'

'How should I know?' Tim spat back.

'Well, it was your idea to come out here.'

'Yeah, but this isn't the kind of thing I've ever seen before.'

'You sure it isn't something you've set up? You know, we go over there to check on your friend, covered in makeup, only to have him jump up and scare us? Seems like something you would come up with.'

Kim knew Tim was about to reply, and angrily, but she was up on her feet before he had the chance.

'Jesus, Craig,' she said, jabbing a finger into his chest. 'What is wrong with you? This is real. You know it is. Can't you smell it?' Ever since they had approached, Kim had been able to detect a tinge of copper in the air. She could smell the blood, and she knew the others could too.

'Well, what do you want me to think, Kim? It's not every day we come across something like this.'

'No,' she said, 'it isn't. Which is why we need to keep our heads.'

Craig turned his cheek and looked to the ground, embarrassed. He nodded. 'Sorry, Tim,' he said.

Tim took a moment before he responded. 'It's okay, this is really fucked up.'

'What do we do?' Ashley said from her crouched position on the floor.

The group was silent for a moment.

'Do we head back?' Kim asked, through it was more of a

statement than a question. That, in her head, made the most sense.

'No,' Tim said, 'we need to reach somewhere with a phone, or at least a signal. The town we're heading towards is the closest to us from here. That's the quickest route we can take to call someone.'

'Yes, but that means moving on through these woods,' Kim said. 'And whoever did this could be waiting here. I'd rather take my chances out in the open, to be honest.'

'Won't help us at night,' Tim said. 'We won't be able to see shit then, either. If we really move and forget about camping tonight, we can hit town at about two or three in the morning.'

'It'll still be dark,' Kim said. 'So we're still in the shit.'

'But—'

'Dammit,' Craig said, cutting off their back and forth. 'Aren't you forgetting something?'

Kim spun to face her boyfriend, surprised and more than a little annoyed at his tone.

'And what's that?'

'Him,' Craig said, pointing to the man who lay on the ground.

'Him?'

'Yes, Kim,' Craig said, raising his voice again. 'We need to check on him. We can't just leave him like this.'

Kim looked at the dead man, who was stone still. Why would they need to check on him? She squinted to see if she could make out any signs of breathing and, if it was there, it wasn't obvious. He was dead, so surely now all they needed to worry about was self-preservation?

'Craig,' Kim said, 'he's dead. We can't do anything for him.'

'We don't know that,' Craig said. 'We can't just leave him like this. We need to know one way or the other. Even if he is dead, we can't just leave the poor guy like this.'

Kim took a deep breath and considered her next words. She could normally bring Craig around to her way of thinking, but when it was something principled—or what he *perceived* to be principled—he could be stubborn as hell.

She was worried that his stubbornness could put them all in danger.

'Honey,' she began again, but he didn't let her finish.

'Kim, how can you be so heartless?'

It took a moment for the words to sink in. *Heartless*? How could he be so ignorant to the situation, the *danger*, they were in? She clenched her teeth, readying herself for a verbal assault, but again she wasn't allowed to finish. This time, Tim stepped in.

'Craig,' he said, gently and calmly, 'I understand what you're saying. I really do. But think it through. We don't know who did this or why. But someone did do it, that we know, and then they hung that thing there,' he pointed to the face, 'for all to see. You don't do that unless there is something seriously wrong with you. Can you really look at all this and say whoever did it won't look to do it again if they find us?'

'There are four of us,' Craig said, as if it made a difference.

'And we don't know how many of *them* there are, Craig,' Kim said. 'Think it through, you idiot.'

'Don't call me an idiot,' Craig said, again turning away, this time to look back at the man.

'Then don't act like one.'

'Guys,' Tim said, 'we need to calm down. Craig, I admire

what you're trying to do, but we can't help that man. He's already dead. The best thing we can do for him is to get the hell out of here, get to town, and call the police. They're a lot more equipped to deal with anything like this than we are. And they're the best chance we have to catch the son of a bitch that did this.'

Craig didn't respond to that, which Kim was thankful for. Though part of her did want him to keep going so she could really get into it with him. The realisation that she wanted that, even in a situation such as theirs, gave her reason for pause.

'So which way do we go?' Ashley asked, getting to her feet. Her face was streaked with tears and her eyes were red, but she was able to keep her hysterics under control for now. Kim put an arm around her. She realised that may have been Tim's job, to offer her reassurance, but fuck it, she had known Ashley for years.

'We go back,' Kim said.

'No,' Tim said, 'we carry on.'

Kim let out a sigh, 'Tim, stop this. We need to go back. I will not stay and die in these fucking woods. If whoever did this is still around, then he could be hiding anywhere. So, we need to get out quickly. And that's back the way we came.'

'The way we came is no safer, and it's a longer trek. If we keep going and stick together, we find help quicker. The sooner we're somewhere safe, the better.'

'Guys,' Ashley said, her voice soft and defeated, 'please don't argue. We don't need that right now.'

'You're right,' Craig said, stepping forward and walking towards the body. 'We need to stop being so selfish and help this man.'

Kim reached for him, as did Tim, but Craig managed to weave between them and jog over to the corpse. Kim could do nothing but follow.

For fuck's sake, Craig, you're going to get us all killed.

6

MORE UNEXPECTED EVENTS.

He'd anticipated the group would have pressed on, quickly, in one direction or another. Either back the way they came, or with any luck, forward.

But this?

The tall, thin, blonde boy was braver than expected. Brave, but so very stupid.

The man silently made his way forward, bare feet feeling their way across the leaves, twigs, and moss, stepping gently as to not make a sound. He settled in behind a thick tree, pushing his body against the bark and peeking around it to watch things unfold. He was maybe twenty metres from them, closer than he would have liked, but in the best cover available.

He grasped the handle of the long blade tied to his thin waist. It wasn't as sharp as it should be; dirty and blunt, useful more for inflicting prolonged pain than doing any decisive damage.

It would still do the trick.

The blonde boy reached the thing he was jogging towards, took a moment to compose himself, and crouched beside it.

The man readied himself.

7

ASHLEY DIDN'T WANT to follow them, her legs didn't feel like they had the strength, but Kim and Tim had run off after Craig, so she had instinctively done the same. Not because she wanted to be any closer to that horrific sight, but because she didn't want to be left alone so far from the group.

Her stomach was cartwheeling and her body shaking, both with adrenaline and fear. She was queasy at what she had seen and just wanted to drop, curl up, and pass out, to wake up safe and sound somewhere.

Somewhere warm, with Tim laying next to her, telling her it was all just a bad dream.

Ashley pulled her phone from her pocket, checking again to see if there was a way to call for help, but the signal was still dead. She was still cut off.

Then they all surrounded Craig, who crouched near the man. And Ashley saw the full acts of depravity that had been committed on him. She wanted to scream again.

Instead, she spun away and clamped a hand over her mouth to stop the contents of her stomach, the *rabbit food*

Kim had complained about so much, from making a re-appearance. As she did, her eyes were drawn to a large tree in her line of sight. She squinted at it, still battling the urge to vomit, but certain she had seen something.

Some kind of movement.

Her vision was blurry from wet, stinging eyes, so she couldn't be sure. It was more than likely further tricks of the brain, considering what they were all going through and, as she looked now, there was nothing. And other than the noise they were making, and the normal ambience of the forest, no odd sounds, either.

'What a fucking mess,' Kim said. Ashley, reluctantly, turned back. She didn't want to take in the details, but she couldn't help it.

The man was big, a similar size to Tim, but with a bald, dirty head. His clothes were old, filthy, and a mismatch of styles, more cobbled together than picked out. Her first instinct was that he might have been homeless, or close to it. No shoes, either, just dirty feet with jagged toenails. All of that was just periphery, though. The real focus of attention was on what had been done to his face.

The skin had been stripped away, leaving jagged edges, obviously cut or hacked from the bone beneath. It hadn't been done with any kind of precision. Chunks of red meat and stringy tendons lined the skull. Without lips, the teeth and gums were exposed in a demented smile. In addition, his jaw hung loose at an unnatural angle, a clear sign it had been fully dislocated.

Then there were his eyes.

Or rather, the lack of them.

In their place were empty, red pits, that bore down inside of his head.

She hoped the man hadn't been alive when he had been flayed.

'Okay,' Kim said, 'you've seen him. He's dead. You know we can't help, so can we please go?'

'Jesus, Kim,' Craig said.

'She's right,' Tim said. Ashley could hear the agitation and impatience in Tim's voice, something she couldn't blame him for. All she wanted to do was run. Maybe Craig was right, maybe that selfishness made her a bad person, and the thought didn't sit well with her, but right now, she didn't care.

'Maybe he has some kind of wallet or identification. We might be able to find out who he is.'

'But why does it matter?' Kim yelled. She squatted down next to Craig, getting right in his face. 'What good can you do here? All you're doing is putting us in more danger.' Her face was going red as she berated him, but Craig wouldn't look at her. 'For fuck's sake, Craig, you can't save everyone.'

'Please, stop shouting,' Ashley said. 'It's too loud. Someone might hear.'

Kim, gritting her teeth, turned to Ashley and nodded. She stood up again. 'You're right, Ashley. But Craig, I'm serious. Pull your head out of your arse and get a move on. Otherwise...' she trailed off.

'Otherwise what?' he asked, still not looking up.

'Otherwise, fuck you. We're leaving you.'

Now Craig looked at her and his expression wasn't pleasant. Even Ashley was taken aback at what Kim had said. Surely she couldn't have meant it, surely it was just the stress of the situation making her lash out, desperate to try and make Craig see sense? It wouldn't exactly be out of character, but still, the way she had said it...

'Go then,' Craig said, with an unnervingly even voice.

'Turn tail and run away. Look after yourself and fuck everyone else. I wouldn't expect anything less from you.'

Not again, Ashley thought, *not now.* This wasn't the time for an argument, this was a time for working together, for looking out for each other. They had to act as one, something Ashley didn't think was looking likely. She looked around the woods again, half expecting to see whoever killed the man spring out from behind a tree and bound towards them with some kind of weapon.

She saw nothing, but still her attention was drawn to that tree. Something about it didn't sit right with her. Had she actually seen something earlier?

A creeping feeling brushed up her spine.

'Guys,' she said, but they were paying her no attention, instead focused on their argument.

'Fuck you,' Kim said, with venom, 'you little prick. Can't you get it through your thick fucking skull that playing the hero is going to get us killed? Who do you think you're helping if you're dead? No one. All you'll be responsible for is putting us in the same position as this poor fucker, because you need to be seen as the do-gooder. It's fucking stupid, Craig. And you know what else? It's boring.'

Craig, ignoring her ranting, reached out a hand towards the man, aiming for the pockets of his dirtied trousers. Before he could dig through them, Ashley saw Tim's hand shoot out and grab Craig firmly by the wrist.

'Don't,' Tim said. It was not a suggestion, but an absolute command.

'Let go of me,' Craig said and tried to wiggle his wrist free. It was futile. Tim's grip looked as strong as iron.

'Enough of this, Craig,' Tim said, sounding more and more assertive with each word. 'I promise you we'll help him, but to do that we need to do the right thing. The sensible thing. We need to get to town and find help. You want to do the right thing? Then we need the person or people who did this caught and arrested. Don't you want that?'

'Of course I do, but—'

'But nothing. That's all there is to it. The man is clearly dead, there is nothing we can do to change that. All we're doing here is messing up what is clearly a crime scene. We need to leave it as intact as possible so the police can do their jobs.' The defiance in Craig's face seemed to slip. 'Come on, man,' Tim went on. 'I really do admire you for wanting to do what you can, but let's just make sure we do something that actually makes a difference.'

Craig was silent for a little while, and Ashley prayed Tim had gotten through to him. Finally, Craig nodded. 'You're right,' he said, sounding sad. 'I just... I just hate the thought of leaving him like this. Of running away.'

'I get that,' Tim said, squatting down next to Craig, releasing his wrist. 'But we've got to look past that. It isn't cowardly if the end result is for the best.'

Again, Craig nodded. Tim put a big hand on his shoulder.

'Oh yeah,' Kim said, her voice still laced with venom. 'Listen to him, but not to your own girlfriend. Fucking prick.'

'Not now, Kim,' Ashley said. She loved Kim, but she didn't want Tim's good work undone. They were close to getting the hell out of here and stupid arguments born from fear wouldn't help with that. Kim clenched her teeth and Ashley could feel the anger radiate from her friend; she obviously didn't want to give up the spat. Thankfully, however, she just shrugged and turned away.

'So,' Craig said, still looking at the poor man. 'Which way do we go? Backwards or forwards?'

He looked to Tim, then up to Kim. Neither said anything at first, and it was Tim who finally spoke.

'I still say we move forward.'

'And I still say we go back,' Kim replied.

Ashley felt herself deflate. One argument avoided, another one incoming.

She wondered if it was just a stand-off of pride between the two, neither wanting to back down, or if they both genuinely believed their point of view was best for them all. Ashley could see both sides of the coin; she wanted to get to safety as quickly as possible, but the thought of staying in these woods for a prolonged period, knowing someone dangerous may still be lurking in here, was a terrifying proposition.

'I say we move forward,' Craig said, still looking at the faceless man. Kim's jaw fell open. 'Tim's right. We should get help as quickly as we can. If that means hiking through here for a little longer, then so be it.'

'You're just saying that to get back at me,' Kim said, folding her arms.

'Yes, Kim,' Craig said, his tone condescending, as if talking to a child. 'The thing first and foremost in my mind right now is to get on your nerves and piss you off. Not to get out of here safely.'

'Prick.'

'Classy as ever, Kim.'

'We don't know what's in here, you idiot,' Kim said. 'Anyone could be hiding in these woods and we would never know until it's too late. They would hear us coming and—'

'If they are going to hear us,' Craig cut in, 'then they've

already done that, because of all the noise we've been making. You yelling like a banshee won't have helped.'

'I wouldn't need to yell if you would just listen.'

'Guys' Ashley said, keeping her voice as quiet as possible, but packing it with as much urgency as she could. 'Enough.'

'So, that's two to one on moving forward,' Craig said. 'What do you say, Ashley?'

All three looked at her.

'Tell me you don't agree with them,' Kim said. 'It's suicide.'

'It isn't suicide,' Tim said. 'It's the most sensible thing to do. Look, Ashley, I know this place, I know how to get us through here quickly. There are more clearings ahead where we can take breaks if we need to. We then move on again to the next clearing. Rinse and repeat.'

'But how long till we're out of the woods?' Kim asked.

Tim shrugged. 'Depends on how quickly we go. If we push it, and I mean really go for it, I'd say no more than six hours.'

'Six hours? That's a long time to be in these woods with whoever it was did that to him,' Kim said, pointing to the body. 'You're crazy.' She looked to Ashley. 'You have to see that.'

Again, everyone's eyes fell to Ashley, and it seemed she was tasked with casting the deciding vote. She didn't like it.

'Look,' she said, holding up her hands, 'I don't know. This is all beyond me. I know we need to keep moving, but I have no idea which way is best.' She looked to the ground and shook her head. 'I just don't know, so don't make me pick.'

'Then it's two against one,' Craig said.

'Bullshit,' Kim snapped back. 'Ashley, now isn't the time

to shrivel away like a mouse. You have a voice, you have an opinion. Fucking use it.'

'You won't be saying that if it doesn't align with what you want,' Craig said. He turned away from Kim, knowing she would yell again, and once more looked at the body. Then, Ashley saw his head cock to the side, like a confused dog.

'Ashley,' Kim snapped, 'will you please grow a pair and think for yourself?'

The comment hurt Ashley, maybe because she saw some truth to it, a truth she didn't want to face, but she was more focused on Craig's growing curiosity. Had he noticed something?

'Guys,' he said.

'Shut up, you,' Kim said. 'You've said enough.'

'No,' Craig replied, 'that's not what I mean. I think...' he stepped forward, leaned in closer to the faceless man.

'What is it?' Tim asked.

'I think he's breathing.'

The collective group held their breath, trying to register what Craig had just said.

'He's breathing?' Ashley asked. 'He can't—'

She didn't finish her sentence. The man suddenly jerked upright into a sitting position with an ungodly roar. His arms quickly reached out and, though they were still bound at the wrist, quickly found Craig's throat and clamped down.

8

The scream Kim had earlier refused to let out now burst free, piercing and unstoppable.

A sense of panic and adrenaline surged through the group as they tried to register what they were seeing. The man, faceless, eyeless, and by rights one who should be quite dead, had his hands wrapped tightly around Craig's neck.

After a moment of surprised inaction, panic set in, and Kim's first instinct was to dart to Craig's aid. Despite the arguing, she found herself by his side before she could even think about it, trying to pry the man's grip loose. Craig's mouth was opening and closing, struggling for breath, but no sound came out. It reminded her of a goldfish out of water, uselessly trying to suck in what it needed to breathe. The crazed attacker made a strained, gurgling sound as he squeezed tighter.

Despite her best efforts, it seemed futile. Kim simply didn't have the strength needed to break the man's hold, so she began clawing at his skin.

'Stop,' she heard Ashley yell. 'Sir, please stop, we're trying to help you.'

It confused Kim. Why was Ashley trying to reason with a man who was, at that very moment, trying to kill Craig? Then it struck her. She looked up to the man's wrecked face, the red holes where his eyes used to be, and realised. He was blind and probably had no idea who they were, so he was fighting out of instinct.

She pulled harder as Craig fought for breath, both of them trying in vain to break the hold. Another thought struck her; *where the hell was Tim?*

She cast a quick glance up to see him standing motionless, his face blank, obviously in shock. But now wasn't the time for that, they didn't have that luxury.

'Hey!' Kim yelled up at him. 'Could you fucking help us?'

Tim seemed to snap back into reality, shaking loose the fog of shock that had him rooted to the spot. He quickly jumped in and grabbed the man's arms. With his added strength, they managed to pull the man's hands away from Craig, who slipped free and began to gulp in large swathes of air.

'Sir,' Ashley went on, 'please calm down. We aren't trying to hurt you.'

The man wriggled and writhed, moaning loudly and pathetically on the floor. They all scuttled backwards from him, giving themselves room as his hands thrust wildly in the air, this way and that, searching for something to latch on to.

'Holy shit,' Craig said, still pulling in much-needed air. His voice was hoarse and croaky.

'How can he be alive?' Ashley asked. Kim had no answer; it didn't make any sense. She helped Craig to his feet and, once up, he bent double, still trying to get his breath. His throat was red, with bruises already forming.

The man continued to thrash about, moaning and gurgling.

'Sir,' Ashley tried again.

'He can't talk,' Craig said, rubbing his neck.

'What do you mean?' Kim asked.

'I saw,' Craig answered. 'When he had me, I could see into his mouth. He doesn't have a tongue.'

'Jesus,' Kim said.

'I think it had been cut out.'

'Poor fucker,' Kim said. 'Someone really wanted to hurt him.'

'What do we do?' Ashley asked, raising the obvious point no one else seemed to be thinking of.

'We keep going,' Tim said, sternly.

'What?' Ashley asked. 'Tim, no. We can't just leave him like this.'

'We have to,' Tim said. 'We're still in danger and we can't help him. Hell, we don't even know if we *should* help him. Did you forget he just tried to twist Craig's head off?'

The man thrashed again, then slowly rolled himself forward onto his knees, forcing the group back farther.

'Maybe he's just scared,' Craig said. Kim was shocked Craig was still giving the man the benefit of the doubt after what had happened. 'Given what he's been through, and not being able to see, he's probably terrified.'

'But we don't want to hurt you,' Ashley said, raising her voice. She was pleading with the man. 'We want to get you help.'

'We can't help him,' Tim said again. 'Do any of you know how to treat wounds like that? Because I sure as hell don't.'

'But he's alive, Tim,' Ashley said.

'For the time being. But for how long? And how long until whoever did this comes back? We can't just wait around.'

'We can't leave him,' Craig said.

'So what now? Do we split up?' Kim asked.

'No,' Tim said. 'Does anyone really want to be the one left behind, just to stand around and watch him in this condition? The plan doesn't change; we still need to go get help. Any way you look at it, we can't help him.'

The man then pulled himself up, first to one foot, then the other, to an unsteady standing position. Kim yanked Craig back a few feet and Ashley and Tim followed suit. Seeing the man at full height, with his grinning, gore-covered face, was as terrifying a sight as Kim thought she would ever see.

The man then began struggling with his bonds, trying to pull his wrists apart and break what was binding them together. Kim saw the thin, metal wire cut deeper into the man's flesh as he did, causing blood to spill from his wrists. If he kept going with that kind of intensity then either the wire would give or, more likely, his wrists would. Given what he'd already been through and survived, she wondered if that would even stop him, and if he wouldn't just keep going till he had hacked right through the bones in his arms.

The man took another step forward and Ashley shrieked.

'Stop,' she pleaded with him. 'We aren't the ones who did this.'

The man's head cocked, as if listening, and his next step was in the direction of Ashley. She shrieked again, and he took another step.

'Everyone quiet,' Kim said, and the man turned his

horrible face in her direction. 'He can hear us.' He stumbled forward a few more steps and the group retreated in kind.

To Kim's eternal annoyance, Ashley the mouse cried out again, and Kim turned to admonish her, to tell her to keep her mouth shut. But Ashley was not looking at the shambling man anymore, she was looking behind them, over to a cluster of trees.

'There's someone out there,' she said, panicked, pointing with a shaking hand.

'What do you mean?' Kim asked.

'I saw someone. A man, I think, hiding in the trees.'

Kim scanned the area her friend was gesturing to, looking as closely as she could, but she could see nothing. And she was still highly aware of the man who was slowly lumbering towards them.

'What did he look like?' Craig asked.

'I don't know,' Ashley said, 'but I saw someone watching us from behind that tree. The big one.'

Kim looked again, to the tree with the thick trunk, one that was easily wider than a person.

'I don't see anyone,' she said. 'Are you sure?'

'I think so,' she replied.

As if things weren't bad enough, Kim was beginning to feel panic take hold even more. If someone was behind them, and this blind, but enraged, man was bearing down in front, that left them stuck in the middle and royally in the shit.

'Do we run?' she asked.

'Not yet,' Tim answered. He began to sidestep his way around the blind, thrashing man, who still gurgled and moaned in a pitiful, yet terrifying way. Kim wanted to believe he was just scared and lashing out, but even so he was a monstrous sight.

Tim motioned for the others to follow his lead, which they did, slowly making their way around so that they weren't trapped between the stranger and the cluster of trees that had so spooked Ashley.

They had almost grouped together when Craig, yet again, took matters into his own hands.

'Sir, can you hear me?' he said, holding his hand out before him in what he thought was a taming manner, like someone trying to calm a wild animal. A useless gesture, given that the animal in question was blind.

'Craig,' Kim snapped, but it seemed he either didn't hear her, or didn't care.

'Please, I want you to calm down,' he said. The man slowly twisted his gore-flecked skull towards Craig. 'Just listen to me. I know you've been through a lot, but the people who did that aren't here, they're gone.' The man started to lurch towards Craig, who matched his slow, deliberate steps in retreat. 'We will help you, I promise, we will get you out of here, but just please try and calm down. Can you understand me?'

The man gave no response to the affirmative, he just continued to follow Craig's voice, bearing down on him. Kim didn't like it. If the man could hear, then that meant he didn't understand what was being said, didn't believe it, or wasn't interested in hearing it. It was that last option that worried Kim, and it was the one she suspected may be true. If a man in a state like his wasn't going to stop, then what good would talking do? A notion hit her; maybe there was a reason they had found him like they had. Maybe he had deserved it.

'Forget it, Craig,' Kim said. 'Tim's right, let's go.'

'Not yet,' Craig said, backing up again. Before he could say anymore, Kim saw a look of surprise flash over his face.

When backing up, he had not been careful where he stepped, and his foot became tangled in an exposed root.

He fell back awkwardly, letting out a yelp of pain as he hit the floor. As he fell, Kim saw that his foot didn't rotate with him, still snagged in the root, and it twisted at a bad angle. Kim didn't hear a snap, thankfully, but didn't need to. She knew his ankle was going to be fucked.

The faceless man clearly heard, and understood, what had happened. He darted forward with wild, almost excited gurgles, and before anyone could react, the previously slow, shambling figure was upon Craig. He clasped his hands together and brought them down heavily onto Craig's face like a club, crushing Craig's nose. The sound of the powerful strike crashing into Kim's helpless boyfriend, and the crunch that followed, made her stomach lurch.

The attacker then dropped onto Craig, once again going for the throat, and began strangling him. Craig tried to squirm and fight, but he was dwarfed and over-powered, like a fish flapping around beneath a bear.

Kim again wanted to help, like she had before, but instinct had been overruled by self-preservation. The man was now on top of Craig and seemed much more dangerous than before.

'Help him!' Kim said, pulling at Tim's arm. Tim didn't move, simply watched. 'Help him, you coward!' Kim said again, hoping to spur Ashley's boyfriend into action. He was a big man in his own right and perhaps the only chance Craig had. Tim turned to look at her, his top lip curling up at the insult she had thrown at him. If she was hoping to provoke a reaction, it seemed she had gotten one.

She just hoped it would be directed towards the right person.

Thankfully, it was. Tim walked forward with purpose,

fists clenched, then broke into a sprint. He ran up behind the faceless man and wrapped a thick arm around his neck, locking in, and yanking back. However, the man didn't relinquish his hold on Craig, whose face was now beginning to turn blue as his eyes bulged in their sockets. Tim gave an almighty, guttural roar and pulled again, harder this time, and finally succeeded in heaving the man backward, away from Craig. Tim's balance gave out and he sprawled to the floor, still clutching the man, who had now fallen on top of him.

Craig rolled away, once again gasping for breath, as the two larger men wrestled and struggled on the ground. Tim still had his arms wrapped around the man's neck in some sort of sleeper hold as the faceless man attempted to slip free. Thankfully, Tim's grip held tight, and he managed to lock his legs around the man's waist, restraining him further.

Craig was free, but now Tim was in a fight, and Kim had an awful feeling that things were about to spiral out of control. Tim needed help, she knew that, but she had no idea what to do. She turned to Ashley, who looked absolutely terrified and was casting nervous glances over to the large tree where she claimed to have seen someone hiding.

'Ashley,' Kim said, grabbing her friend by the shoulder, trying to get her to focus. 'We need to help him.'

Ashley tensed up. Kim knew her friend was scared, she was as well, but they couldn't just stand by and leave Tim to it. It may have taken some prodding, but he had stepped in and saved Craig. Eventually, to Kim's relief, Ashley nodded.

'What do we do?' she asked.

Kim had no answer, but she pulled Ashley along behind her and ran over to Tim and the stranger nonetheless.

The faceless man was writhing with a renewed vigour,

and Kim couldn't understand, considering his injuries, how he still had the energy and strength. He managed to drive a hard elbow into the ribs of Tim, who let out an audible cry. Tim's grip loosened slightly, which seemed to be the opening the man needed. He slipped from Tim's grasp, swivelled, and was quickly atop him, now in the dominant position, and began clubbing at Tim with his clasped hands, like he had done to Craig. Tim brought his hands up to his face for protection, but the blows found their mark. The terrifying man seemed to act with an almost renewed rage, and Kim was sure that the gargled nonsense the man was spewing was now more focused. It was almost as if he was trying to speak, but what he was saying was completely unintelligible.

Now that the man was free, helping Tim was going to be much more difficult, if not impossible. She knew Ashley was thinking the same thing, but Kim was not about to give up.

Then she saw it, close to where Tim lay struggling as he tried to avoid the repeated blows the faceless man rained down. Laying amongst the dead leaves was a thick branch. Kim ran to it and heaved it up, feeling its substantial weight. If she swung it hard enough, then the man was certain to feel it.

She hoisted it back, preparing to strike, and built up a primal scream in her gut, ready to unleash it at the same time as the blow in order to exert every ounce of energy she possibly could.

But the makeshift club was snatched from her grasp.

Shocked, she spun to see Craig holding her weapon. He was on his feet, red-faced with one hand on his neck, and he was balancing on one leg.

'What the fuck are you doing?'

Craig ignored her and hobbled past, making his way over to the attacker and Tim. He brought the club up and swung at the man.

Kim wanted to scream at him and how useless he was. Craig's aim was poor, and any power he tried to exert was clearly hampered by his injury. The strike connected feebly with the man's back. Given the size of the club, it still landed a heavy hit, but it served to do no more than irritate the faceless man.

Kim's aim would have been for his head, as hitting him full force there would have given Tim the best chance of escape. It may have killed the man, but better that and saving Tim than what Craig had accomplished in only angering the attacker further. The man turned and lurched forward, grabbing wildly in Craig's general direction.

And it was enough.

Yet again he found Craig, who cried out, and pulled him to the ground. He crawled over Craig like a spider covering its prey. Yet again, Craig had landed himself in a dangerous position, but this time Kim had half a mind to leave him to it.

'Please, no,' Craig pleaded and fought back, hitting out at the man. It made little difference, and he soon had Craig pinned beneath him. He straddled the young man and again began to club at his head.

Kim looked around; the branch Craig had wasted now lay under him, jutting out from under his back, out of her reach without getting too close to the faceless attacker.

As much danger as he was currently in, Kim couldn't help but curse her boyfriend. His fuck up had screwed them all. No, scratch that, his three fuck ups had screwed them all. If he had just left the man alone, or let her take the swing, then they would have been able to get away. Still, as useless as he was proving to be, leaving him wasn't an option.

She readied herself again, about to dive in with nothing but her bare hands in order to help her boyfriend. But before she did, she saw Tim get to his feet, his face bloodied and full of anger.

'Tim,' Kim yelled, 'we get him together. Ready?'

But Tim wasn't listening.

Soon, she saw why.

He strode towards the faceless man and heaved up what was in his hands. A weapon of his own; a large, angled rock. One that took two hands to hold.

'Tim!' Ashley yelled. 'No!'

Tim ignored her and brought the rock down into the back of the man's head with incredible force. The sound of impact—a dull thud with an audible crack—was sickening. The faceless man's head lolled and his arms dropped to his sides. He remained motionless for a second before eventually flopping face first into the dirt. His body twitched on the ground as Craig scrambled free.

Tim moved to stand over the man and again brought up the rock, holding it high above his head.

'Tim, stop!' Ashley cried.

But Tim didn't stop. Instead, he brought the rock down, again and again, onto the man's fragile head, screaming like an animal as he did.

They could hear the faceless man's skull crunch and crack beneath each blow. A messy hole formed in the back of his head, exposing grey and red mush beneath, mush that spattered out after each strike. The head cracked and split further into a sickening mess.

Finally, Tim stopped and dropped the bloodied rock

carelessly to his side. His eyes were wild with fury and he took quick, shallow breaths.

‘My God,’ Ashley said, her voice trembling. ‘What have you done?’

9

SHIT.

He had been careless.

The girl had seen him.

He'd been too greedy in his curiosity, wanting to know everything that was going on, and he'd assumed they would all be too engrossed in what they were seeing to look back towards him.

He'd been wrong.

That assumption may have cost him everything.

The redhead *had* looked back and, even though he'd pulled back as quickly possible, she'd spotted him. Worse, she had alerted the others.

A fucking stupid mistake, and one that could ruin everything. If things went to shit, and one of them died before he got them back, then he would be made to suffer for it. He may even be denied his feed.

The family all liked their food alive and aware, as he did. As it was meant to be. Dead meat didn't have the same effect, the same taste. If he brought back cold meat, then Father and Mother would make him feel it.

Hell, the whole family would.

Thankfully, it might not come to that.

Things had developed, enough to draw their attention, and the group was forced to fight for their lives. It had allowed him to slip from his position behind the large tree and into a thick section of undergrowth.

Once he settled into place and was sure he was out of sight, he drew out his blade. As penance for his mistake he pushed the dull metal into the meat of his thigh. There was some initial resistance before the blade sunk in, drawing forth a stinging pain.

He then twisted the blade more, wanting to cry out, but knowing he couldn't.

His eagerness had nearly cost the family.

Father always said that impatience was a weakness. That it was something they needed to fight.

He knew this impatience, this craving, was something that would only grow stronger the longer they went without feeding.

And it had been so, so long since they had indulged. Long enough that the family were now close to tearing each other apart, or trying to, just to appease a fraction of their desires.

They had a chance now, though, a chance at fresh meat, and he would be damned if his impatience was going to cost them that.

He watched the events unfold. The savage act of a skull being crushed, exposing the ruined brains beneath.

He smiled and ran his tongue over dry lips, following the split that branched off up towards his nose.

The carnage excited him.

It made him want to run out and join in the fun.

But he couldn't do that, not yet.
He had to abstain.
For now.
His time would come soon enough.

10

ASHLEY WAS ROOTED to the spot, unable to move, scarcely able to comprehend what she'd just witnessed.

How could she look at Tim, the man she'd just told she loved, in the same light again after what he'd done?

Tim wasn't a killer.

Yet there he stood over the body of a man who now had a large, ugly hole in the back of his head. One that Tim had caused.

The situation had been dire, granted, but were his actions justified? The first time he brought the large rock down had been shocking enough, but it was what followed that really scared Ashley. The man was down after the first blow, helpless it would seem, but Tim had kept going. The anger on his face as he did so, that pure animalistic fury, was like nothing Ashley had ever before witnessed.

'What have you done?' she asked again, her voice quiet.

Everyone looked at Tim, who was finally slowing his breathing into a steady rhythm. As he did, some tension seemed to release from his body.

'What was I supposed to do, Ashley?' he asked. 'Didn't

you see what was going on? He was going to kill us. He was about to kill Craig.'

'But... but,' Ashley struggled to put into words what it was that scared her. She felt a hand on her shoulder and turned to see Kim standing beside to her.

'It's okay, Ashley,' she said. 'It's over.'

'It's over?' Craig said, pulling himself up to his feet. His voice sounded ravaged, like he had been smoking a hundred cigarettes for half a century. 'A man is dead,' he added and cast an accusing glance at Tim.

'And you would have been, too,' Tim said, 'if I hadn't acted. Because I'm sure as shit no one else was going to do anything.'

'You didn't have to kill him, though,' Ashley said. 'That was... it was... just savage.'

'I'm sorry,' he said, throwing his hands up into the air, 'am I missing something? You do remember that he wasn't stopping, right? Nothing we said slowed him down. He just kept on coming. You remember that, don't you, Ashley? We tried to talk him down. We tried to run. But we still ended up in the shit. Do you think I wanted to do it? You think I woke up this morning thinking, *gosh, I really hope I get to kill someone today*? For fuck's sake, get a grip. What do you suppose I should have done?'

Ashley had no answer. Well, that wasn't true, she did have an answer. Once the man was down after the first strike they could have all just run. That would have been enough. But no, Tim continued and crushed the man's skull. She didn't know how to vocalise that, though. Or rather, she didn't want to.

'It's just...' she began, but trailed off, deciding instead to remain silent. She looked to the ground.

'I did what I had to,' Tim said with an air of finality, like that was the end of the subject. But Craig wasn't as willing to let things drop, it would seem.

'No,' he said, 'you went too far.'

Tim turned to Craig and marched up to him, making the smaller man shrink back.

'You,' Tim said through gritted teeth and jabbed a finger into his chest, 'nearly got us all killed. Twice.' He then shoved Craig back, punctuating his point with a physical exclamation mark.

'Bullshit,' Craig said.

'He's right,' Kim cut in.

'Excuse me?'

'For fuck's sake, Craig, what the hell was that? First, you had to go and examine him like you're some kind of forensics expert. Then, you tried to talk him down, as if you had any idea what you were doing. And to top it all off, even after the fucker tried to rip your head off, you wasted a clean shot to help Tim and ended up in trouble again. Three fucking times we could have just run, and three times we had to pull you out of the shit.'

'No,' he said, but Kim just held up a dismissive hand and turned to Ashley.

'Honey, I know that was scary,' she said, 'but Tim is right. That situation was beyond fucked up. I don't know what was wrong with that man, maybe he was just scared and fighting for his life, but regardless, he was still trying to kill us.'

The words did make some kind of sense to Ashley, somewhere in her brain, but still, in her gut, it didn't sit right.

But the fact was they still needed to get out of here, and Ashley was still aware of what she saw, or thought she saw, behind that tree.

'None of it matters,' she said, putting her concerns into words. 'We need to get out of here. Quickly.'

'Agreed,' said Tim, but he didn't look at her.

'Yeah,' Kim echoed. 'Whoever did this to him might still be out here.'

'Hang on,' Craig said. 'Ashley, didn't you say you saw someone?'

Ashley pointed over to the tree. 'Yes. Over there.'

What she'd seen hadn't been much, but it had been enough.

Enough to be certain.

A face; peeking out from behind the tree trunk, which in and of itself would have been bad enough, but it was how the face looked that really horrified her.

'Only one person?' Tim asked.

Ashley nodded. 'I think so.'

'Should we go check it out?' Kim asked. Ashley didn't like that idea. 'There are four of us, we'd have the upper hand. Surely it's better to know.'

'You getting a taste for this, Kim?' Craig asked her.

'What do you propose?' she shot back. 'What if there is someone there?'

'*If* someone's there?' Ashley asked. 'I know what I saw, Kim.'

'I know, honey, and I believe you. Which is why I think we need to be sure. If we need to deal with something, then I'd rather we do it when we're ready for it.' She turned to Tim. 'What do you think?'

Tim took a moment, then let out a sigh. 'You might be right.'

'I'll go,' Craig said.

'No,' Kim said and grabbed hold of his jacket. 'You've done enough. We all go together. So wait.'

She then walked over to the body of the dead man, near to where Craig had just been lying, and grabbed the heavy branch that he had wasted earlier.

'All tooled up now, are we?' Craig asked.

'Better than giving it to you,' she said. 'Now let's move.'

Ashley was reluctant, but she knew it had to be done. Kim was right; if someone was watching them, then chances were the person had malicious intent. Otherwise, why not come out and show themselves? Especially after what had just happened.

The four of them grouped up and slowly made their way over to the tree. Ashley shivered as they walked, both from the dropping temperature as darkness set in and also from the horrible sense of foreboding that was worming its way up from her gut.

She felt bare and exposed and scared. She wasn't a fighter, never had been, and hated any kind of violence. On that front, she and Craig were very much the same. Still, she did wish she had some kind of weapon to hand, even if it only served as a show of force. She quickly scanned the ground for something to use, but found nothing.

In short order, they stood before the large tree. Its circumference was wider than Ashley's arm length, its height dizzying. It was immense, dwarfing any other tree around it, and Ashley noted its aged and worn bark.

'Anyone there?' Kim asked loudly. There was no response. Only the eerie noise of the woods; the chirps and tweets of whatever wildlife lived here.

'If you are there, don't move,' Craig added. 'We won't hurt you.'

'If we don't need to,' Kim stipulated. She turned to the others. 'Okay, on the count of three, we go. Ready?'

Ashley tensed up; she wanted things to slow down, but Kim carried on the count.

'One. Two. Three.'

Kim and Craig sprinted round the tree first, and from their reaction alone Ashley knew there was no one there. Kim's frown had quickly melted away to confusion.

Ashley ducked around and saw for herself; no one was hiding. No one was waiting for them, ready to leap out. There was no man with a cleft lip.

The face she thought she had seen wasn't there.

They were alone.

'I was certain,' Ashley said, the first to speak. 'I know I saw someone.'

'Well,' Craig said, 'they aren't here now.'

'Maybe they ran off,' Ashley said.

'They might have,' Kim said in a tone Ashley couldn't read. She didn't know if her friends believed her or not, and that bothered her.

'I'm not lying,' Ashley said. 'And I'm not confused. Someone was there.'

'Well, we need to deal with the here and now,' Tim said. 'They're gone, so we can't do anything about it.'

'Agreed,' Kim said.

'And I say we stick to the original plan and get out of here,' Tim finished.

'But do we agree on which way to go?' Craig asked, looking between Kim and Tim.

Kim took a moment, then nodded. 'Yes. We follow Tim. He knows the way, so we get to town as quickly as we can.'

Tim looked a little taken aback—they all were—but nodded and smiled his thanks.

'Let's go,' Tim said. 'We'll make town before you know it.'

'Then what?' Ashley asked, a new worry dawning on her.

'What do you mean?' Kim asked.

'When we get to town? Then what?'

'Then we get help,' Craig said as if it was the most obvious thing in the world.

Ashley nodded. 'Okay. And what do we tell them?'

'We tell them what happened,' Craig answered.

'Really? Do we tell them how that man died, then? How his head got bashed in like that?'

To that, no one had an answer, and the reality of Ashley's point sunk in.

'It doesn't change anything,' Tim said eventually. 'We get help and we tell the police what happened. Everything that happened.'

'But what'll happen to you?' Ashley asked.

'I don't know,' Tim said with a shrug. 'What will be will be. In my view, it was self-defence, but if the police see things differently, so be it. I'll deal with the consequences.'

'Tim,' Ashley began, but he cut her off.

'It's okay,' he said, holding up a hand. 'It's the right thing to do. And the situation isn't exactly normal. But right now, we need to focus on what's important. We need to move. Everyone agreed?'

It seemed everyone did agree, keen to just keep moving, but Ashley was worried. Worried that things were never going to be the same again between them. And she was worried about Tim. It was an honourable gesture, to own up to what had happened like that, but she still couldn't forget what he had done, and the look on his face as he had done it. Would he really be so eager to face up to any consequences that would come?

For the next few hours they walked on in silence, and

the darkness grew deeper. Keeping their footing was difficult, and progress was slow due to Craig's injury. His ankle had swollen badly, and they'd had to stop numerous times for him to rest. Tim said it looked like a sprain, not a break, but Craig still couldn't bear much weight on it. It slowed their progress considerably, but Tim shouldered his weight and helped him along the whole way.

Without complaint, Ashley noted.

As more time passed, she began to feel more and more guilty for judging him so quickly. Yes, his actions had been extreme, but they had been in an extreme situation. She made a mental note to talk to him the next chance they got, to try and figure it all out.

What little light there was in the woods began to wane drastically, so much so that vision was becoming an issue.

'Do we switch on the flashlights?' Craig asked.

'It could draw attention,' Kim answered.

'It could,' Tim agreed, 'but we won't get far if we can't see where we're going. I don't think we have much choice. We only need put on one, keep it to a minimum. I'll take the lead, because I know where I'm going, and I'll have the light. The rest of you just follow my footsteps.'

Tim pulled out his mag light, which was big and heavy enough to be a useful weapon in itself. She was surprised he hadn't thought of using it earlier. They still had Kim's large branch, but Craig was using it as support, not that it really helped.

The beam from Tim's light punctured the growing darkness and illuminated a small spot off in the distance. He arced it around to scan the area up ahead, and they began to move again. As they moved, Ashley watched the beam of light sway this way and that, fully expecting the light to reveal that horrible face again, staring at them from behind a tree.

Waiting for them to walk right up to him.

It made her shudder.

As well as the dark, the cold was getting worse too. They all wore thick, waterproof jackets fit for hiking with layers underneath, but even so Ashley could feel the chill of the night seep into her bones. The sounds of the forest changed, too, as the nocturnal animals came out to play.

'How long till we stop?' Craig asked, breathless, clearly struggling. Tim was helping him along up ahead, leaving Ashley and Kim walking in a pair just behind. Another thing that Ashley didn't like; being at the rear. The whole time she was expecting to feel a pair of hands grab her shoulders and yank her off into the shadows. Every so often she would cast a glance behind to see if she could see anything, but there just wasn't enough light left to be of any use. Someone could have been not ten feet away and she wouldn't have know. Not unless they made a sound.

'There is a clearing not too far ahead,' Tim answered. 'Somewhere we can take a break and rehydrate. Just keep going a little longer, okay?'

'Yeah,' Craig said, 'no problem.' The strain in his voice indicated that it was a problem, but he pressed on regardless, hopping and hobbling as quickly as he could.

They moved on for another ten minutes before Craig spoke again.

'What's that?'

'What?' Tim asked.

'There, up ahead,' Craig said. 'Just past those trees. Is that a house?'

'There aren't any houses out here,' Tim said and pointed

the flashlight in the direction Craig was pointing. 'I'd know if... holy shit.'

Ashley could see it faintly illuminated by the light of the torch, up a small incline in the distance. The beam only showed a small area, giving sight to the corner of the wooden structure.

There was indeed a house, standing alone out here, dark and ominous.

'Tim?' Ashley asked.

'This isn't right,' Tim said, looking perplexed.

'What do you mean?'

'I mean there are no house here. I've walked this route dozens of times and this has never been here.'

'It looks pretty old,' Kim said. 'And the trail leads right up to it.'

Ashley and Kim walked up beside Tim and Craig. Ashley could see that Tim's expression was one of pure confusion.

'Did we take a wrong turn somewhere?' Craig asked.

Tim shook his head. 'I... I don't know. I don't think so. I guess we must have.'

'And you're sure you've never seen this before?' Kim asked.

'Never,' Tim answered. 'I think I'd remember it.'

He let his beam swoop over the house so they could take in all the details.

It was two stories high, with a wide canopy over an entrance door and dirty windows to the front elevation. It was built almost entirely of old timber that had warped and aged. The only change in construction material lay on the sagging roof; mismatched slate tiles. There was a porch area that ran the full length of the front of the house, enclosed by wooden railings that had eroded over time, leaving gaps in their perimeter. Whilst not quite in a state of disrepair, it certainly felt aged and forgotten.

'Do you think anyone lives in here?' Kim asked.

'Doesn't look like it,' Craig said. 'Looks abandoned.'

'Looks creepy,' Ashley said.

'So, do we go around it?' Craig asked.

'Of course,' Kim said.

Tim took a step forward. 'Actually,' he said, 'I think we should go in.'

11

'ARE YOU FUCKING NUTS?' Kim asked, unsure if she had heard Tim properly. 'What possible reason could we have to go in *there*?'

'Craig is in bad shape,' he said. 'And we need to take a break anyway. Why not get out of the cold?'

'What happened to the plan of pushing on and only stopping in clearings?'

'This looks clear enough to me.'

'But we don't need to go inside,' she said. 'If we need to take a break, we can just do it out here.'

'What if there's someone in there?' Ashley asked.

'It doesn't look like it's been lived in for a while,' Craig said. 'Seems empty.'

'We don't know that,' Kim said. 'Hell, it could even belong to that guy who was missing his face.'

Kim was just throwing out excuses as to why they shouldn't go in. Not that she should have needed them, surely common sense dictated they stay away?

'Or maybe whoever hurt him lives here,' Ashley added,

which was another good point. 'It might belong to the man I saw.'

Just hearing that made Kim's skin crawl. The thought of someone out there, keeping tabs on them, watching their moments, gave her the creeps. She hugged herself tightly and looked around the area, seeing nothing but darkness between the trees.

'If you even saw someone,' Tim said.

Kim saw the hurt in her friend's eyes. *This fucking trip has been a catastrophe,* she thought to herself.

'I did see someone,' Ashley said.

'Regardless, we keep going,' Kim said. 'That was the plan before, so are we agreed now?'

'No,' Tim argued. 'I'm going in, and I'm going to see if there are supplies or anything else we can use. There might even be something we can use to bandage up and support Craig's ankle. Hell, they may even have means to contact town.'

'Oh come on,' Kim said, throwing up her hands in exacerbation. 'Can you see any phone lines around? We're in the middle of the fucking woods. There's no phone in there.'

'I'm still going in,' Tim said. 'You can all wait out here if you want.'

Kim couldn't believe what he was saying. It made absolutely no sense. Worse yet; he actually started walking up the incline towards the house.

'Are you fucking nuts?' she said. He had been as eager as she was to get out of here, now he wanted to stop and take a look around?

'Tim,' Ashley pleaded, 'please come back.'

'Come with me,' he said, without looking back. 'It'll be okay. I promise.'

Kim heard rustling and saw Craig fishing his own flashlight from his backpack, juggling with the heavy branch he had being using as a makeshift walking aid.

'Tell me you aren't going as well?' she asked.

'I'm not leaving you,' he said, 'but if he's going in there, then we're going to need a light.' He clicked on his beam and shone it up to Tim, who kept moving forward.

'What do we do?' Ashley asked.

Kim wanted to tell her that they would just carry on, that Tim could go to hell, but the truth was that he was the only one that really knew the way out of here. They could follow the trail, sure, but if it deviated or branched off and they picked the wrong direction, then they had no hope of getting out of here tonight. If at all.

'We either go in after him or wait out here until he's done,' Craig said.

The three looked at each other, considering their options.

Tim was at the front entrance now, shining the beam through the glass section of the door.

'What do you see?' Craig called up to him.

'Looks empty,' he called back. Kim saw his hand reach up and take hold of the handle. She held her breath as he twisted it.

The door slowly swung open.

He turned to face them, waiting. 'Coming?'

'Fuck it,' Craig said. 'We're better off together. Let's be honest, if someone does want to hurt us, we have a better chance with him.'

That didn't sit well with Kim, but she knew Craig might be right. It *was* Tim who had saved them from the faceless man, as much as Ashley might not like the way he had done it, and there was a chance they would need to see that side of him again. Separating from Tim wasn't going to help their chances.

'Yeah, fine,' Kim said, letting out a sigh, 'Let's go. I still don't like it, though.'

She dug out her own flashlight and clicked it on. Ashley followed and did the same.

Craig turned to Tim. 'We're coming up,' he yelled. Tim gave them a thumbs-up and rested his body against the jamb of the door.

'You know, Ashley,' Kim said, 'I can't really weigh up your boyfriend. He can swing from being a hero to an absolute prick in an instant.'

Ashley didn't respond.

They made their way up to meet Tim and, as they approached, Kim saw the house in closer detail. The guttering was loose, and in some cases hanging off completely, and the timber slats that horizontally lined the walls were faded, some sections completely overgrown with a dark mould.

She also noticed a horrible, sour smell.

The whole place was like something time had forgotten, left behind to fester and ruin.

Kim shone her beam through one of the large windows, the one farthest to the left-hand side of the house, and saw what appeared to be a dining room inside. It was cluttered with old furniture; a sloping bookshelf lined one of the walls, half-filled with books, and a large dining table sat in the middle of the room with a filthy tablecloth over it. It looked to be ornate lace, maybe once of good quality, but now ragged and stained. Plates were set around the table, some with food left on them.

Raw animal meat of some kind.

And it looked relatively fresh.

'Hold on,' she said, piecing it together. 'Someone does live here. Look.'

Ashley peered in beside her.

'They've been eating,' Kim said.

Craig looked in next, hobbling up next to them, using the thick branch as support. 'Doesn't seem like it has been sitting out too long. Someone was eating something here fairly recently.'

'I don't like it,' Kim said.

'We'll be quick,' Tim replied, sounding impatient, and entered the house.

Kim sighed, trying to restrain her anger. 'Prick,' she muttered.

They followed Tim inside and entered into an open hallway area. Running up to the first floor was a set of stairs that at one time could have looked quite grand. Now they looked as creaky and aged as the rest of the house. The internal doors were all bare timber that was also withered and worn.

'Now what?' Craig asked.

'We look around,' Tim said, seeming impatient.

'So where do we start?'

Tim shrugged. 'I don't know.'

Kim shook her head. 'You don't know? You were eager enough to get in here.' Wanting to get it over with, she chose the door on the right-hand side of the hallway and pointed. 'That one,' she said. 'We start in there.'

Craig led the way, hopping forward. Each time he landed, a dull echo from the hollow floor reverberated through the house. If they wanted to keep things quiet, then they were out of luck. Craig pushed open the door, slowly, and it creaked as it opened. They huddled together and entered what appeared to be a library or study of sorts.

A large, heavy-looking bookshelf stood against the wall opposite the window, and the remaining walls were lined with shelving. Old looking books, some leather-bound, some little more than clumped together scraps of paper, filled the case and shelves. Clearly, the residents were voracious readers, or liked to pretend they were.

There was also an old writing desk and single chair set next to the window. The desk top was littered with piles of paper that seemed filled with sketches and notes, as well as an open book or journal of some kind.

'No one in here,' Kim said. 'And nothing we can use.'

She turned to leave, but Craig slowly made his way inside.

'Hold on,' he said, scanning the room.

'What?' Kim said. 'It's just junk.'

'These books aren't like anything I've ever seen before,' he said, sweeping the beam of his torch along their spines.

'So? They read rubbish, big deal.' Kim just wanted to move onto the next room already, then get the hell out of here.

'Some are foreign. Not even a language I know.'

'Again, big deal. There are loads of languages you don't know. Hell, sometimes even English escapes you.'

'Funny,' he said, still looking over the bookshelves.

'All right, Craig,' Kim insisted, 'let's go.'

Thankfully, he seemed to listen to reason and, rather reluctantly, followed them out of the room.

'Now where?' he asked.

Kim thought it pointless to look in the dining room; they had viewed that from outside and had seen nothing of use or value, other than plates of raw meat. As hungry as she was, Kim didn't see herself eating that. 'Let's go to the back,' she said. 'The kitchen is probably through there. If they do have any first aid or anything, that might be where they keep it.'

She looked to Tim to lead the way, but he simply stood aside and gestured, rather grandly, for her to go first.

'Not really a gentlemanly move, considering the circumstances,' she told him. He didn't budge, though, so she shook her head and continued on, past the stairs and to a set of double doors that led to the back of the property. She carefully pushed the doors open to reveal a mess of a kitchen. Units that were perhaps once white were dingy and yellow, drawers and cupboard doors missing. Crusty, dirty plates and dishes were piled up on the countertop, and beside them sat a chopping board and large knife, both stained with blood.

Stepping farther inside brought them into a big, open area that lined the back of the house. The kitchen connected to a second dining area with another table; this one filled with junk.

The horrible stench Kim had detected upon entering the house increased tenfold, and Kim brought her hands up to cover her mouth.

'What's that smell?' Ashley asked.

'Something's rotten,' Craig said.

'I think I'm gonna throw up,' Kim added, meaning it. Her stomach was churning.

'Let's just be quick,' Ashley said, prompting them to look around.

Rifling through the kitchen units, Kim could find nothing of interest, only cutlery and kitchenware—most of it aged and almost antique. All of it horribly, horribly filthy. How anyone lived in such a way was beyond her. A window overlooking the back of the house sat above a large steel sink, and she crept towards it with a horrible feeing someone was out there. She cast her torchlight out, worried she would see someone standing there, but saw only the dark, ominous woods.

'This is pointless,' she said.

'Just be patient,' Tim responded, sounding annoyed.

'This is interesting,' Craig said, drawing their attention. He was standing over the far side of the room, resting on the upturned branch, looking into an open door.

'What is it?' Kim asked. They all made their way over and looked through the open door.

Kim gasped.

The room was a shrine of death; animal bodies hung from the ceiling, cut from throat to genitals, their empty stomachs pulled wide open, revealing where their insides once were. They were deer mostly, but the bones of some smaller animals littered the floor.

'That's horrible,' Ashley said. 'Those poor animals.'

'Well,' Craig said, 'people have to eat. But I'm more interested in that.'

He pointed beyond the animals to the back of the room, to something that Kim had also noticed. There was another door, in effect making the room little more than a squat corridor, but the door was not like any other they had seen in the house. It was made of strong-looking oak, and the fact that it was chained shut was very troubling.

'Yeah,' Kim said. 'Very weird. It doesn't matter, though. We've looked and can't find anything, so let's leave.'

'Yeah,' Ashley said. 'I definitely agree with that.'

Kim pulled at Craig's sleeve, trying to pull him back, but he stared rapt at the door. He cocked his head a little.

'Come on,' she insisted.

'Yeah,' he said. 'It's just...'

'Just what?'

Then Kim heard it, too, and her body froze.

It can't have been.

'What is it?' Ashley asked.

Kim listened intently, hoping and praying she wouldn't hear it again, but somehow knowing she would.

And she did.

This time, they all did.

'Oh my God,' Ashley said with a soft, shaky voice. 'Jesus Christ.'

Kim had no words.

She just wanted to get the hell out of there and run, but she knew instantly that they were going to have to find a way to get that door open, as much as she really didn't want to.

The sound came through again, muffled by the door, but still clear enough to hear.

It was the sound of a child.

Crying for help.

'Hello?' Craig yelled.

The cries and sniffles ramped up, triggered by Craig's voice. They then turned to eligible words.

'Please,' the child's voice said, 'I need help. I'm trapped down here. They have me trapped. Please let me out. Please. I'll be good, I promise.'

'Fuck,' Craig said, still trying to grasp what was happening.

'What do we do?' Ashley asked.

Kim already knew the answer. Whereas before, when they had seen the faceless man, her instinct had been to run and leave him, but this was different. They had to get in there, somehow, and help. This was a child, so there was no way they could leave him here. Her mind raced, thinking of what kind of monster would keep a child prisoner. Perhaps the same kind who would rip off a man's face and leave him for dead. Hell, maybe it was that man himself, maybe Tim had been right to bash his head in. Still, she felt panicked. The events of earlier scared her, made her feel like she was in danger, but now it felt like the danger was here, that it was imminent.

The chains on the door looked thick and strong, even if they had rusted a little. They all wrapped together around a single, large padlock. Without a key, getting access would be tricky, if not impossible.

'Please help,' the boy pleaded again, and then said something that made Kim's heart rate spike. Words that confirmed to her they were all in terrible, immediate danger.

'They're going to eat me.'

12

Ashley was terrified.

She couldn't really make sense of what they'd all heard. On the one hand, it was simple, a child was trapped in there and he needed help. But *what* he'd said, that was what didn't make sense. Not in the real world. Hearing that, coupled with what they'd already experienced today, made her want to give up, drop down, and assume the foetal position.

'We need to get in there,' Craig said. He dropped the branch and began pulling uselessly at the chains.

Ashley knew he was right, but she couldn't get past what the boy had said.

They're going to eat me.

What was a sane person supposed to do with that? Her thoughts jumped back to the faceless man they had found earlier. Considering the state he was in, Ashley had little doubt the residents of this place were the ones responsible. And it *was* more than one person, Ashley was sure of that now, because the boy had said so. He had used the plural.

They.

No wonder the man, without eyes or a face, had been so eager to fight. For all he knew, he was fighting for his life.

Which meant they all were now.

The clanking of the chains drew Ashley back to the moment, but Craig was making no headway.

'So how do we get in?' he asked desperately.

'I think we leave it,' Tim said.

All three turned to face him.

'You can't be serious,' Craig said. 'Jesus, Tim, there's a kid in there.'

'Leave it alone,' Tim said, almost ignoring Craig's comment. 'There's nothing but trouble down there.' He stepped away, back into the kitchen. 'Come on,' he said, waving them toward him. 'Let's keep looking.'

Ashley couldn't believe what she was hearing. She again thought back to the words she and Tim had shared earlier and how happy it had made her. But he was not the same man she thought she was in love with.

It seemed Tim was not that man at all.

Perhaps he never had been.

'We aren't leaving a kid in there,' Kim said.

'You should listen to me,' he said. 'If you'd have listened earlier, we wouldn't be in this mess.'

'No,' Kim said, 'we are not abandoning him.'

'There has to be a key,' Craig said, turning back to the task at hand. 'For the padlock. Maybe it's close by.'

'We should search the kitchen,' Kim said.

The three of them filtered out of the small room, and Ashley noted that Tim wouldn't even look at them as they passed. She stopped next to him.

'Tim,' she said. 'How can you be so careless?'

'How can you be so stupid?' he answered coldly.

The comment stung. 'I... I don't understand. Help me to understand. What's going on?'

'Like I said. You didn't listen to me before. And you're ignoring me now. So, if you're all so eager to bring more trouble down on you, go right ahead.'

'But it's a child,' she said. 'And it was you that wanted to come in here in the first place.'

He just shrugged. 'I don't like it,' he said and walked away, back to the hallway door. She thought he was going to walk through, but he simply leaned against the jamb like he had done outside.

She couldn't understand him, and her mind was reeling, but she knew she needed to focus on the immediate issue. They needed to find the key, if it was here, and get the hell out.

She joined Kim and Craig in their search, sifting through drawers and cupboards, searching frantically. Ashley had a feeling they didn't have long before whoever lived here returned.

Come on, she prayed. *Come on, come on, come on.*

Then she pulled open the bottom drawer, one filled with scraps of paper, old photos, and other junk. As she pushed around the rubbish, she saw it slide into view; a large, iron key.

She snatched it up. 'Is this it?'

Craig quickly hobbled over. 'Might be,' he said, taking it from her grasp. She and Kim followed him back over to the door, but Tim stayed where he was.

Craig put the key to the lock and, thankfully, it slid into place easily. He jiggled and turned it, and the loop at the top sprang open.

'It worked,' he said, pulling away the lock and dropping it to the floor with a heavy thud. 'Just hold on,' he yelled through the door. 'We're coming in to get you. We'll get you out of there, buddy, I promise.'

The child didn't respond at all, and that didn't sit well with Ashley, but she was too concerned with getting in there to give it too much thought.

She watched as Craig quickly pulled the chains loose, and they dropped to the floor alongside the padlock. He wasted no time pulling open the door, and a breeze of cold air hit them. Through the door, in the darkness, Ashley could make out a set of creaky wooden steps running down into the black void below. A wave of sickening stench rose up and hit them.

'Hello?' Craig yelled down. His voice echoed, but no one responded.

'Little boy?' Kim added. 'We opened the door, you can come up. We'll get you out of here.'

Still nothing.

This seems wrong, Ashley thought to herself.

'I'm going down,' Craig said.

'Wait,' Ashley replied, instinctively grabbing him.

'What?'

'Why isn't he responding?'

'I don't know,' Craig said, 'but that's why I'm worried. Maybe he's really hurt.'

'It's just... isn't it strange?'

'This whole thing is strange, Ashley,' Craig said. 'In fact, it is beyond strange. But that doesn't mean we leave a little kid down there.'

Ashley nodded and looked to the floor, embarrassed, and felt her cheeks flush. How could she let fear override her compassion like that, especially towards one so innocent and helpless? They'd all heard the little boy's cries, so there was no doubt he was down there.

Even so, given the boy's silence, and Tim's reluctance to help, and his warning to leave it all alone, something seemed very wrong to Ashley.

'I'm going down,' Craig said. Despite the brave gesture, Ashley saw it plastered all over his sweaty face; he was scared as well.

'No,' Kim said. She bent down and plucked up the heavy branch that Craig had earlier dropped. 'We go together. Ashley, you coming?'

Ashley closed her eyes, took a breath, then nodded.

And so they descended. Craig took the lead, slowly creeping down the steps with his torch lighting the way. The stairs were simple wooden slats, but because there was no handrail, Ashley felt off balance, like she could easily fall over the side at any moment. The beam eventually found a dirt floor, and as it swept up, she could see that the walls surrounding the basement were stone. Not shaped or carved, but random sections wedged together in wire mesh casing, holding back the ground outside. Streaks of old and new water lined the stone, and it was clear that whoever lived here felt no need to damp-proof the area.

Craig swept the beam around the room, looking for the child, but instead found something else.

Something horrible.

Ashley took a sharp intake of breath.

If she had been scared before, what she saw here took things to a whole new level. It was reminiscent of the room upstairs, the one where animal carcasses hung from the ceiling.

Things hung from the ceiling here, too, but they were not animals.

These dead things were once very much human, all

strung up and hanging upside down. Those that still had arms had their hands bound together.

'What the fuck,' Craig uttered.

After seeing the morbid scene of death and desecration, Ashley doubled over and vomited.

The hanging bodies were in various stages of decomposition, and some were so stripped of flesh that they were little more than skeletal. Where flesh still remained on others, it had withered and yellowed. The skin on the heads had shrunk, pulling back over the skull, lips twisted up into a grimace. The eyes, where there were eyes, bulged out from sunken eyelids.

Some of the bodies were men, some were women, but worse, some were...

Ashley vomited again.

'We need to get out of here,' she heard Kim say, her voice now small and quiet, like a scared child.

Craig didn't reply, but she could hear him start to hyperventilate.

Ashley got to her feet, legs feeling like they were going to melt away beneath her, and took Kim's hand. 'Let's go. Now.'

'But...' Craig said, casting around the beam of light, 'where's the—'

He didn't finish the sentence, because the beam stopped on another monstrous sight. This one standing in the corner of the room.

And very much alive.

Ashley screamed at the hulking monster that stood so tall it had to hunch over to fit beneath the basement ceiling. It must have been over eight feet tall, grotesquely fat and bulbous, wearing little more than rags. Where pectorals should have been, swollen, bloated pockets of fat spilled over the rotund gut. Whatever it was, it was disgusting, the repulsion made worse by its face, which looked cherubic.

The thing was mostly bald, with only small tufts of fair hair scattered about its scalp. It had big cheeks and tiny, beady eyes. Its mouth, however, looked wrong. Too large, too wide, and as it pulled back its lips into a smile, Ashley saw that its yellowed teeth were short and stumpy.

'Oh look,' it said in the same childlike voice they'd heard through the door. 'People have come to play.'

13

THEY WERE in his home now.

The family home.

This was good.

He'd worried things would go wrong, especially after he'd been seen earlier, but everything had worked out well for him. However, he was confused at the silence. If they were inside, then he should be able to hear them screaming; a symphony of pain and terror. Had the family left the house unattended?

Regardless, at least they were inside, trapped like flies in a web.

Helpless.

Waiting to be devoured.

They just didn't know it yet.

Then he heard a faint scream that seemed to come from the basement below.

A lopsided smile formed over his cracked lips.

They knew it now.

He surveyed the area and saw the rest of the family

silently making their way through the trees towards the house. Father saw him and waved.

He was excited now, truly excited, almost giddy.

This was it.

Now it was time.

14

THE HULKING FIGURE took a heavy step forward. As it did, Ashley saw rolls of fat drop down over his ankles.

'Goodie, goodie,' it said, still with that childlike voice. 'Come to Henry.'

Ashley screamed again, and Kim joined her. Craig looked horrified as well, but was making no sound. They all began backing up.

The monstrous man lifted an inhumanly heavy arm and pointed a fat finger at Craig.

'You,' he said. 'You get to play first.'

That was the catalyst for them all to flee as one. Turning on their heels, they rushed for the stairs, bolting up them as fast as they could. Craig, with his injured ankle, was slower, but both Ashley and Kim made sure to each take a hand and drag him along. Kim threw the thick length of wood she had been carrying at the thing, but her throw was weak and it didn't reach its target.

They clattered up the stairs, feet hitting the timber with loud thuds. The wood creaked ominously beneath them, and Ashley prayed the stairs didn't break and send them tumbling down below to be trapped with that thing.

She could hear it waddle quickly after them, its footsteps a mix of shuffling and heavy slapping as its bare feet hit the dirt.

She allowed herself a look over her should and saw the thing that called itself Henry was already at the bottom of the stairs, smiling up at them, as if all of this were some kind of game.

'Can't run,' he said. 'Nope. Can't, can't, can't. Nowhere to go.' He licked his lips, sloppily, and began his ascent. The three of them spilled through the door at the top and Kim slammed it shut. They heard the beast run quickly up the steps with loud thuds, seemingly moving far too quickly for something of that size.

Craig thrust himself against the door to brace it. 'Help me,' he said.

Ashley and Kim both pushed against it as well, readying for the force that was about to work against them.

'Tim,' Ashley yelled, 'we need help.'

She turned to look back into the kitchen, expecting to see him still leaning against the door frame, but he was gone. 'Tim,' she yelled again, louder this time.

The booming footsteps reached the top and stopped.

They all waited.

The handle slowly turned, and the door pushed against them gently. Craig pushed back, clicking the latch back into place.

They heard the hulk laugh from the other side of the door. It was a disturbing, high-pitched titter. Like a child enjoying an exciting game.

'Can't keep me in here,' he said. 'Ma and Pa tried, but

you've let me out. They won't be happy, but the chains are off now. That means I'm allowed to come out.'

All three tensed up and readied themselves.

But it was useless.

The door was shoved open with such force they were all thrown to the floor and slid out to the kitchen. When Ashley regained her orientation, she looked up to see that the door was open and Henry was coming through. He almost looked too big to fit through the frame, and her heart raced as she hoped he would be, but those hopes were crushed as he hunched down and squeezed himself through with a grunt. They all backed up as quickly as they could and got to their feet as Henry began to advance towards them.

'What do we do?' Kim asked, frantic.

Henry laughed again, another excitable titter.

'Run,' Ashley said. 'We have to outrun it.'

'Oh,' it said, still smiling. 'Are you going to hide? Should I come find you? Sounds like fun.'

Ashley had experienced many different levels of fear over the course of the day, but what she was seeing now eclipsed all that.

'Fuck it,' Craig said, 'run.'

They turned and bolted, but the thing was quick to react. It squealed in delight and bounded forward, moving quickly across the kitchen. Ashley and Kim managed to get through the door to the hallway, but heard a gasp, then a scream.

They turned to see that Henry had hold of Craig, one arm wrapped around his waist. The brute quickly hoisted the blonde man up like a rag doll. Or, Ashley thought, like a kid holding a teddy bear.

Henry began to laugh excitedly.

'See,' he said. 'I told you that you would be first, little man.'

He laughed again and began to bounce up and down, shaking Craig as he did.

'Help,' Craig screamed, kicking wildly, his feet not even touching the floor. 'Please, help me.'

His face was pale and his eyes were wide in absolute fear. Ashley had never seen a human look so terrified in real life.

'Craig!' Kim yelled, horrified.

Ashley didn't know what to do. It had been scary enough when the faceless man had grabbed Craig earlier, but this? This was something else. There was absolutely nothing they could do to help Craig against the giant freak of nature.

Henry then turned Craig, who was still dangling in mid-air, to face him, and wrapped another bulbous arm around him. 'Want to know what I do when I catch people who try to hide?' Henry asked.

'Please,' Craig begged. 'Just let me go. I won't tell anyone about this place, I promise. Leave us alone and we will never come back.'

'But I don't want you to leave me alone,' Henry said. 'That would make me angry.'

'Just don't hurt me,' Craig said.

'Hurt you?' Henry asked, feigning confusion. Then a mischievous smile formed over his lips. 'You mean, like this?'

He squeezed Craig suddenly and violently, pulling his arms in tight like a bear hug, engulfing Craig into his mass. Craig let out a horrible shriek of agony and the monster laughed even more. It slowly relaxed its grip, but, even so, Craig still screamed and writhed. He began to cough violently.

'Please,' he pleaded weakly. 'Let me go.'

Ashley had no idea what kind of damage had been done, but the thing seemed incomprehensibly strong. He might have cracked Craig's ribs, or worse.

'No,' it said, its face turning into a frown. 'So stop asking.'

'Please,' Craig begged. In response, Henry squeezed him again, eliciting more screams.

'You'll make me angry,' he said, before again easing up. 'Just like my brother did, and you should have seen what I did to him. So, if you don't want the same to happen to you, then you need to shut up. And do what I tell you. Okay?'

Craig was just a whimpering mess, and he dangled helplessly from Henry's grasp. Henry squeezed yet again, causing more howls of pain.

'I said, *okay?*'

'Yes,' Craig answered as tears streamed down his face. 'Yes, yes. Okay.'

'Good,' Henry said, a smile returning to his face. 'If you're good, then I might let you pick out your own place to stay in here. Most of the others in the basement just get put wherever. Won't it be nice to choose where you live?'

Ashley thought of the bodies of the dead that hung from the ceiling in the basement, and Craig must have realised the same thing. He began to weep, drawing more laughter from the enormous hulk.

'They always cry,' he said and then looked over to Ashley and Kim. 'You will too. Both of you.'

They both took a step back.

'Don't leave me,' Craig begged, seeing their movement.

'Oh, don't worry,' Henry said. 'They aren't going anywhere. If they try, I'll catch them too. You'll all be together here with me and my family.'

'And where are the rest of your family?' Kim asked.

'Out looking for my brother,' he said. Then added, in a conspiratorial whisper: 'They won't find him, though. When they asked where I left him, I lied.'

He laughed, evidently pleased with himself.

'What do we do?' Ashley whispered to Kim. A recurring question, she realised, since entering these damn woods.

Craig was staring at them both through tear-filled eyes, and he began to sob loudly, pleading with them to help him. Or at the very least, not abandon him. Ashley's stomach knotted up. She knew there was nothing they could do for him, and they'd die if they tried. So, did that mean she had already decided to leave Craig for dead? Was she that selfish and careless?

And, if the situation was reversed, she wondered if the others leave her as well?

'Tim?' she called out, yelling out of pure desperation. She didn't know where the hell he was or what he was doing, but he was the only hope she could think of. If any of them had a chance of saving Craig, it was Tim. They needed the same person who had so sickened her earlier, the person who had smashed the man's head open with a rock.

She couldn't agree with what he'd done. In fact, it downright scared her, but she needed him now. They all did. Hell, seeing the danger they were all in, maybe he had been right in his actions.

But Tim didn't answer. He had seemingly abandoned them.

Ashley heard Henry's childlike laugh again.

'Okay,' he said. 'I guess it's time for me to catch you two as well.' He lifted Craig up before him like a toddler. 'You, stay here.'

With that, he kept one arm around Craig's back, but put

the meaty forearm of his other against Craig's chest. In one, sudden motion the monster tensed, curling one arm in and pushing the other out.

Ashley jumped at the sound of the sickening crack as Craig was instantly bent backwards. This time, Craig didn't just scream, he wailed. His cries were so loud, so raw, it sounded as if he would continue with ever-rising intensity until his heart gave out. Henry had a big smile on his face, obviously pleased with his work, and dropped Craig to the floor like a sack of meat. Craig continued to scream and scream and scream, barely taking a breath. His eyes were wide, and Ashley saw veins pop up in his throat and forehead as his face went bright red.

His arms and legs twitched slightly, but he didn't move.

'No!' Kim yelled. 'Craig!'

Craig's only response was to continue screaming, staring at nothing. Ashley couldn't comprehend what kind of pain he was in, but it was enough that he had lost all notion of them even being there and was only able to focus on the pain. No words, just a long, continuous, guttural screech.

Ashley grabbed Kim's hand and pulled her back, knowing if they had any chance of survival, they needed to run.

Now.

Sobbing, Kim resisted Ashley, taking half a step towards her boyfriend.

'Baby?' she said. Craig gave no response, just continued with his screams, over and over.

The thing then took a big stride forward, over Craig, and planted a large foot onto the floor.

'He won't be going anywhere,' Henry declared. 'Now, which one of you wants to come see me first.? He grinned, running a fat, wet tongue over his thin lips.

Kim then gave up any resistance and let Ashley pull her away. The two girls sprinted through the hallway, to the entrance, and spilled out of the still-open front door.

Then the girls stopped dead with a shriek.

They weren't alone.

15

THE SURROUNDING AREA, dark before, was now illuminated by flaming torches held by a group of people who stood outside of the old house.

The residents, Ashley guessed.

There were four in total, all of them standing still, patiently watching the girls. They didn't look surprised in the least to see them.

Ashley felt like Goldilocks getting caught red-handed by the returning bears. These bears, though, seemed distinctly more sinister.

A man and woman, the oldest-looking of the group, stood centrally between two others. The man had a big, bushy grey beard, and his skin was as pale as ash. The hair on his head was scraggly and patchy, in contrast to the thick beard that covered the lower portion of his face. One eye hung considerably lower than the other, and she could just make out through the facial hair that he had a severe cleft lip, one that split up to his bent nose. He wore a faded shirt beneath dirty blue overalls.

The woman next to him, roughly in her fifties, was short,

stout, and sturdy. She wore a petticoat and apron, and she had grey hair fixed up in a bun. Her checks sagged and her face was littered with small, angry-looking growths and lumps.

The two on either side were younger. Next to the oldest man stood a girl, who looked to be in her thirties, and was painfully skinny, almost skeletal. Her dirty blonde hair was thin, showing scalp, and one eye was completely white, without any pupil.

Lastly, there was another man, and Ashley realised immediately that it was his face she had seen earlier, peeking out from behind the tree. He was also lithe, though his bare arms were quite defined, and Ashley saw that he only had three fingers on each hand. All but him held a flaming torch above them; thick sticks wrapped in cloth at the head that had been set alight.

The glow from the torches cast an eerie, flickering yellow hue over the group.

'What do we have here?' the oldest man asked in a gravelly voice.

'You been in our home without permission?' the woman, who Ashley presumed was his wife, added with a sneering smile.

Ashley still heard the booming footsteps of that beast, Henry, as he thudded towards them from behind. Ashley and Kim quickly ran left, towards the far side of the porch, as the giant man squeezed himself through the door.

'Damn it,' the eldest man said, 'did you let him out?'

The hulk laughed.

'Now, Henry,' the older woman said, 'you lied to us. David wasn't where you said he would be, was he?'

'Ma, David had it coming,' Henry said.

'We'll deal with this later,' the man said. 'Ted told us

where you left your brother, but right now we have other matters at hand. After all, we don't want to be rude to our new guests.'

'Of course,' the old woman said, 'where are my manners?'

'Who are you people?' Kim asked.

'We live here,' the man said, taking a step forward. He scratched at his beard. 'That's our home you were walking around in, as if you owned it.'

'We're sorry,' Ashley said. 'We didn't know, we just—'

He cut her off with a dismissive wave of his hand. 'My name is Benjamin, or Ben. This here is my wife, Adela. That young man is Ted, and the girl is Claudia.' The young woman gave a clumsy curtsey.

'Very good, Claudia,' the mother said. 'Always good to show manners.'

'And that,' Benjamin said, pointing to the brute in the doorway, 'is Henry. But I think you may have already met. We're the Webb family.'

That name sounded horribly familiar to Ashley, and she recalled the urban legend Tim had told earlier. But that was just a story, it couldn't really be true, could it?

'Let us go,' Ashley said. 'Please, just let us get our friends and leave. We won't tell anyone about you. Or what happened here.'

'And what did happen here?' Ben asked.

Kim jumped in this time, with anger in her voice. 'You killed people. You have them strung up like meat in your basement. Or left in the woods to die, like the man whose face you ripped off.'

Ben straightened up and looked to his wife. She shook her head and looked over to Henry, who laughed.

'Seems we have a bit of a problem,' the man said.

'Whether you plan to tell anyone about us or not, well, that don't really matter.'

'Yeah,' the younger man, Ted, said. 'See, been a long time since we had visitors.'

'Too long,' Adela agreed.

'And we like to be good hosts,' Ben said. 'Can't let you go just yet. Not without putting on a good, hearty meal.'

'We aren't hungry,' Kim said.

'Doesn't matter,' he replied, smiling. 'You won't be eating.'

The family all erupted into laughter, as if what he had said was the funniest thing in the world. Ashley felt her stomach drop to the floor, and she couldn't stop from shaking.

'Been a long time since we ate,' Ted said.

'There seems to be plenty for you to go at in the basement,' Kim argued. Ashley heard her friend's voice break, fear cutting through the anger. She looked over to Kim and saw tears streaming down her face.

'Old meat,' Ted said, dismissively. 'Not much good to us anymore. We have a certain need and are very particular about our food.'

'Yeah,' Adela chimed in. 'It really has to be warm.'

'And squirming,' added Claudia, speaking her first words of the morbid conversation.

'Please,' Ashley begged. 'Please, just let us go.'

Ben again rubbed his beard. 'You mentioned getting your friends. Who were you talking about?'

'There's another one inside,' Henry said. 'But he ain't going nowhere.'

The father nodded and looked to Ashley. 'And who else?'

Ashley paused. She had no idea where Tim had fled to, and she was angry, furious, that he had abandoned them, but if he was about to get away, she didn't want to alert them to that. Maybe he could get help, if they could just survive for long enough. Right now, it looked like their only hope

'No one,' Ashley said. 'Just us.'

'Aw,' Ted said. 'That's sweet. A lie though, ain't it?'

'No,' Ashley said, then stopped. Of course he knew it was a lie, he was the one who had been following them for God knows how long. He knew about Tim. Hell, he'd probably watched as Tim cracked open the faceless man's skull.

'We know there's someone else, silly girl,' Ted said. 'Mind telling us where he is?'

'I don't know,' Ashley said, 'honestly. He ran while we were still inside.'

'Rather cowardly,' Ted said.

'Very,' Kim added.

'Can't stand a coward,' Ted said. 'He seems to have let you all down.'

The worst part about Ted's cruel taunts was that he was absolutely right. The brave, honourable man she thought she knew, even if it had been for a relatively brief period, obviously didn't exist in the real world; he was just a facade. A cover used to hide the real Tim, the coward beneath.

Given his actions, she wondered if she could really hold out any hope of him contacting the police at all, or if he would just keep the whole thing quiet and let them die, all so that he wasn't held accountable for what he'd done.

It seemed Kim had been right about him; the man was a prick.

'I'm here,' a voice said, one that Ashley recognised. She turned to see Tim appear from around for the far side of the house. He stepped up onto the porch.

'Tim,' Ashley called.

'It's okay, I'm here,' he said. He kept walking towards them.

Initially, Ashley was thrilled, but suddenly she realised Tim was getting too close to Henry's massive form. What was he planning? He couldn't take on the brute, surely? Then Tim stopped, just beside the beast.

Henry made no move to attack.

'Tim?' Ashley asked. Her mind was scrambling to make sense of what was going on. Something didn't seem right. The whole family again burst into riotous laughter.

Tim included.

'What's going on?' Kim whispered to Ashley.

'Sorry,' Ben said. 'Seems we have one more introduction to make. But, like Henry here, I think you've met this one before as well. In fact, I think you know him pretty intimately. This is our youngest, Timothy.'

The group laughed again and Tim gave a big, theatrical wave. 'Hi, girls.'

16

ASHLEY'S HEAD WAS SPINNING, unable to comprehend what she was hearing.

It didn't make any sense. It couldn't be true. None of this could be true. She felt light-headed, then her legs gave out and she dropped heavily to the wooden floor of the porch.

'What the fuck are you talking about?' Kim asked incredulously.

'Exactly what I said,' the oldest man said. 'Timothy here is one of us. Always has been.'

'Come on, Kim,' Tim said. 'You're a bright one. Work it out. Do you think it was an accident we ended up out here?'

'You didn't even know about this place,' Kim said. 'You were as confused as any of us when you saw this fucking house.'

Tim just shook his head. He actually looked disappointed. 'Nope, not confused, just acting that way. You were all really easy to fool, by the way. You know that? All I had to do was come into your boring little lives and play the perfect boyfriend for Ashley. Then I planted the seeds for a small trip away, to get to know each other a little better, for

Ashley's sake. All with the hope of becoming one big, happy group of friends.'

'Just to get us out here?' Kim asked.

'Of course,' Tim said. 'See, not a lot of people come into these woods. It's pretty rare we get visitors who wander by of their own accord. Whether they realise it or not, people subconsciously avoid this place if they can help it. Didn't you feel it when we crossed into the woods? That happens for a reason, and it's been getting stronger and stronger over the years. Good for protection, not so much for visitors. So, we needed to be a little more creative with things, and getting people to come visit us out here is my job.'

'And one you do well, every time,' Ben said. 'You do us proud, boy.'

'Thanks, Dad,' Tim said, gushing like a schoolboy.

'You fucker,' Kim said through gritted teeth.

Tim shrugged. 'Always had a mouth on you, Kim,' he said. 'But I do like your spirit. Truth be told, it was a shame it couldn't have been you that I used. I think we'd have had more fun than I had with the little mouse on the floor over there.'

'Fuck you,' Kim said. 'I'd never let you anywhere near me.'

Tim laughed. 'Well, not now, obviously. But I saw the signs. I'm good at reading people, Kim. You and Craig aren't even together anymore, not in any real sense. Boyfriend and girlfriend? You two are a joke. How long has it been since you two actually liked each other? How long since you, you know?' He made an 'O' with his thumb and forefinger on one hand, and thrust the forefinger of his other through it.

'Go to hell,' Kim said.

'More insults. But I notice you didn't answer or try to deny it. Face it, Kim, if I'd have tried, I could have had you.

And I wanted to, believe me. You're much more my type. But it would have made it difficult getting you all out here if I'd have come between whatever was left of you and Craig. The more people I bring home to meet the family, the better. No offence, but they'd have been most disappointed if I'd just turned up with you. You're a pretty girl, and in good shape, but not exactly enough to fill a family of eight.'

That confused Ashley, and it pulled her back from the mental abyss she was about to fall into. 'Eight?' she asked. 'There are only six of you.'

'Only six of us here,' Tim said.

Great, Ashley thought. If, by some chance, they did get away, then there were two more of those freaks running around out there somewhere.

Unless they were in the house and had been the whole time.

Kim grabbed hold of Ashley, pulling her to her feet. 'Get up,' she whispered.

'Oh,' Claudia said. 'Getting ready to run, I think. Reckon you can get away? Think you can outrun us?'

Tim snorted a laugh. 'You can try, girls,' he said. 'But it would be useless. This is what we do.'

'What?' Kim asked. 'Kill innocent people?'

Tim shrugged. 'A family's gotta eat.'

'Then eat fucking vegetables. Or deer. Or rabbit. Or anything but fucking people. How sick do you have to be to do this kind of thing? How did it even start?'

Tim rolled his eyes. 'Bit of a long story, that. One I'm not sure you'd believe.'

'Try me,' Kim said, pulling Ashley back a bit farther. There was a small gap in the porch railing behind them, Ashley noted, and she knew what Kim was planning.

'No,' Tim said, 'I don't think so. You're stalling now. The

shock has worn off, a little, and now you're just playing for time.'

'I'm trying to figure out what's wrong with you people,' Kim said. 'I mean, look at you. What's wrong with your faces? Is it some kind of inbreeding?'

They all laughed again, like hyenas. 'Well,' Tim said, 'now she really is hurling out the insults.'

'Indeed she is,' Benjamin said. 'What do you take us for, animals? We ain't sick like that.'

'Then why do you look so... so...?' Kim trailed off.

'Why do we look the way we do?' Ben asked, finishing her words. Kim nodded. 'Bit of a side effect to what we do. That's all.'

'So,' she said, pointing to Tim, 'how come he doesn't look like the rest of you?'

At that, Tim's smile fell. Of all the insults Kim had thrown, Ashley realised that one genuine question had actually struck a nerve.

'All right,' the father said, taking another step forward, 'I think we've talked for long enough. Can only talk for so long before everything is said that needs to be said. Only one question left; are you gonna make this easy for us, or are you gonna run and make us work for our supper?'

'Don't forget Craig,' Tim said to the girls, scowling. 'Wouldn't want to leave him behind. Think what would happen to him.'

Ashley knew what Tim was doing, but regardless, it was working. Leaving their friend behind was still weighing heavily on her, but no matter which way she looked at it, Ashley just couldn't see how they could help him. It made her sick and ashamed, but she knew they had to try to save themselves.

It seemed Kim was in agreement.

Ashley felt her friend quickly pull her away, hard enough that she almost lost her footing. They slipped through one of the gaps in the railings and bolted off into the woods.

Ashley heard whooping and hollering from the family behind.

'It's settled,' she heard Benjamin yell. 'A hunt it is.'

17

THE PAIN CRAIG felt from his spine was unlike anything he'd ever experienced before. Every breath, every twitch of muscle, caused it to flare up in an eruption of white-hot agony.

He knew, without question, that his back was broken.

Would he ever walk again?

Would he ever move again?

Hell, would he even live long enough to care?

The floor of the kitchen on which he lay was filthy. He could see small animal carcass, rats or mice, under the stove; a long insect, a millipede, crawled over one. Funny the details you notice when your mind is about to break.

Craig had managed to stop screaming, mostly because his throat was too sore to carry on. Instead, he simply moaned and mewled between breaths.

Tears still rolled down his cheeks, but he couldn't allow himself to fully sob, as the movement was too painful.

So he wept motionless.

In silence.

As much as he could hope for a miracle, deep down he

knew it was pointless. So, his mind, whether he wanted it to or not, was now coming to terms with his impending death.

How had it all come to this?

The weekend was supposed to be a new start for him. He had planned to rekindle things with Kim, to show her they were meant to be together and get things back on track. Also, they were supposed to be bringing a new friend fully into the fold, one who seemed to make Ashley happy, and Lord knows that had been a long time coming.

The trip was supposed to be the start of a new chapter, a positive one.

But it had turned into something straight out of a nightmare.

No, worse than that, because you woke up from nightmares.

It was real, and its effects were permanent.

It had all started when they'd entered these woods and found the man with no face. And from there, things had only gotten worse.

Finding this house. Finding the basement.

And the thing in the basement.

The hulking beast that called himself Henry didn't make sense to him. He was just *too* big, both in height and girth. Surely, no human could be that big and still walk around so easily? His strength, too, seemed inhuman. The way he had snatched Craig up so effortlessly, like he was weightless, was terrifying.

Craig remembered how the grotesque thing had squeezed him, pushing him into its rubbery, sour smelling skin. He was sure some ribs had been cracked, but the whole thing had seemed like a game to Henry. And then the hulk had, quickly and simply, snapped Craig's back, like it was nothing.

Craig could hear voices outside, one of them Kim's, and one that sounded like Tim's as well, but there were others too. Unrecognisable. Perhaps the people that lived here? It was as good a guess as any. He thought of Kim and Ashley running away, leaving him behind as Henry stepped over him.

Like he was nothing more than dirty laundry on the floor.

Seeing his friends flee so quickly, seeing his girlfriend leave him behind for dead without even looking back, hurt every bit as much as the physical pain he'd been put through.

Did he mean so little to Kim?

Then again, if he was honest with himself, he had a huge part to play in them being in this hellish situation anyway. He was the one who had insisted on going to check on the faceless man. He was the one who had insisted they try to talk that same enraged man down. On top of that, when he had seen Kim ready to swing the heavy branch, aiming squarely at the man's head, Craig's instinct was to stop that. He knew the damage it would do and didn't want Kim to have a person's death on her conscience. So, had taken the responsibility of protector on himself, taking the weapon from her and aiming it at the man's back and ribs, hoping to avoid any permanent damage.

It hadn't helped.

It had just fucked things up further.

Even after all that, all that he had done, when they had heard the child's voice through the door in the kitchen, he was the one who had insisted they find a way in, even though Tim was adamant that they leave well enough alone. Craig, again, had thought he knew best. Regardless of what anyone else thought, his way had to be right.

And look what it had unleashed.

Maybe his friends were right to leave him behind. If they did make an escape, they were probably better off without him.

He would only hold them back.

His thoughts were broken by excited yelling from outside; something was happening. He heard a male voice say something about a hunt. Then, quite clearly, 'Go get them.'

A few moments later, he heard multiple footsteps enter the house. One set in particular, booming and thunderous, was very recognisable.

'Where is he?' a male voice asked.

'Kitchen,' Henry answered. Craig still didn't understand why his voice was how it was; so high-pitched and childlike. He was clearly fully grown, overgrown if anything, so why did his voice reflect that of a child?

The footsteps moved towards the kitchen, and Craig held his breath as people entered. The first to appear was a man with a beard who smiled when he saw Craig. A woman with her hair in a bun followed, then Henry squeezed through the door. All of them looked odd, unnatural in some way. Henry's oddities were obvious, but the man had a gap in his top lip that ran up and met a disjointed nose, and the woman seemed to have drooping eyes and horrible growths all over her skin.

But there was one more person who entered. One that made no sense to Craig.

Tim.

He smiled and waved to Craig. 'How's it going, buddy?'

Craig tried to speak, but the effort hurt. All that escaped was a low moan.

'He looks a little confused,' the man with the beard said.

'Then he can stay confused,' Tim said. 'I'm not explaining it all again.'

'He's a handsome one,' the woman said, stepping closer to Craig. Her dirty boots stopped just before his face. 'Wonder if I should have a little play with him before we get going.'

There was a flash of something as—whatever was thrown—struck the back of her head. A plate crashed to the floor close to Craig and shattered.

'You don't need to play with the likes of him,' the bearded man yelled.

'Did you just throw something at me?' the woman roared in response. She stomped over to the kitchen units, grabbed an old, iron kettle, and launched it across the room at the man. It hit him in the face, knocking him backwards. 'Don't you ever do that again, you piece of shit.'

She then ran at him and began swinging hard punches at the man, alternating between the ribs and head. The man tried to block, but too many got through, and he again stumbled backwards.

Henry was laughing heartily. His disgusting mass jiggled like jelly, clearly enjoying the show.

Tim was cackling as well. 'Get him, Ma.'

'All right,' the man said, still trying to fend off the continuous assault. 'All right, I'm sorry,' he said. 'Will you stop?'

The woman eventually did, but the scowl on her face remained. She landed one more shot as the bearded man straightened up to his full height, bringing her knee up into his crotch. Upon impact, the man let out a groan and doubled back over.

'Don't ever throw shit at me again,' she yelled and stomped back over to Craig. He tried to shuffle away, but only succeeded in flaring up the pain in his back. 'And you,' the woman said, 'stop fucking moaning.'

She pulled a leg back and let loose with a kick, hitting Craig directly in his already injured ribs. He let out a howl as unimaginable pain exploded inside of him. Through it all, he was also aware of a warm feeling spreading over his groin as he wet himself.

The group just laughed at his suffering.

'Henry,' the man said, still holding his injured groin. 'Get him ready. Might as well have dinner prepared for when your siblings get back.'

'Okay,' Henry said, happily, and began walking towards Craig.

'And if you pull any shit like this again, I swear we'll lock you in that basement for good, and you'll never eat again. Or maybe I'll even take you to see Grandpa, see if he can't straighten you out. How does that sound?'

Henry's eyes went wide. 'Fine, I'll be good,' he said. He turned to look down at Craig. 'Let's get you downstairs.'

Craig held his breath as Henry reached down for him with giant, filthy hands. Craig knew the obese monster was going to pick him up, and he knew any movement was going to hurt. He braced himself for the pain, which came in waves as he was hoisted up and slung over the behemoth's fat shoulder. Craig cried out, unable to help himself.

'Come back up when you're done,' the man said, obviously the father of the deranged group. 'If the twins aren't back within the hour, we are gonna get started without them.'

'No problem,' Henry said and began to walk, each step causing Craig more and more agony.

With all he had been through already, part of Craig just wanted it to end. Thoughts of escape and freedom were futile; he was utterly broken. A quick death seemed like the best he could hope for.

But he knew the chances of that one, small mercy were non-existent.

He fully expected more suffering.

And he was to be proved right.

18

KIM'S LEGS burned from the effort she was exerting as she and Ashley sprinted through the trees.

The ground was uneven, and gaining traction at speed was difficult. More than once, one of them had taken a tumble. Ashley had fared a little better, but with the slippery moss and tripping hazard of exposed roots, they weren't moving as fast as they needed to.

Worse, with no natural light, vision was almost non-existent, and only the thin beam of their flashlights guided the way. She couldn't hear anything behind them, but knew they were being followed. Kim remembered what the thin man had said as they escaped.

We'll make this fair. You have a full ten-minute head start. Then, we track you down.

His arrogance sickened her. She had a feeling, however, that in this environment, it was a confidence that was probably justified. The girl had chimed in too, laughing dismissively as she spoke.

You don't have a chance, you pair of bitches. Gonna get what's coming. We're going to find you both, then have our fill.

They continued their taunting as Kim and Ashley fled. Kim didn't know exactly how long it had been since they'd begun their attempted escape—the concept of time and its passing was now lost in a mix of adrenaline and a need to survive—but she had a feeling that ten-minute mark was fast approaching.

If it hadn't already passed.

They were both breathing heavily, and Kim could feel her chest starting to burn. Each breath also caused a stabbing pain in her side.

Ashley was coping better with the physical exertion, Kim noted, but it wasn't surprising given her keen interest in sports. She was, however, on the verge of tears. Kim could hear it in her breathing.

'Which way do we go?' Ashley asked, her voice wobbling.

'We need to find our way back to the trail,' Kim said. 'Then we can follow it back out of here.'

'If we don't get lost.'

That was a good point. Tim had taken the lead the whole trip, so they really had no idea which way they were supposed to go.

'First we need to find the trail,' Kim said. 'That's all we need to worry about for now.'

'I have an idea,' Ashley said and changed direction slightly, pulling them left.

'Why this way?' Kim asked.

'We approached the house almost head on, up an incline, right?'

'Yeah.'

'And we set off running at about ninety degrees from where we came in. So, we need to angle back left again and we should come across the trail.'

Kim was impressed. The girl was clearly in a fragile state, hell, they both were, but when confronted with a problem, she had managed to think logically and come up with a plan. Normally, it was left to Kim to act in any kind of situation, let alone one where they were fighting for their lives. Maybe the extreme danger had kicked the mouse into fighting mode. Kim was pleased with that, because they would need to fight to get out of this hell. She followed Ashley's lead without hesitation, and both pushed themselves on as hard as they could.

Kim knew the two lunatics who were following would have no such trouble making their way through the trees. This was obviously their home, their environment, a place they knew well. Kim and Ashley were the fish out of water here, trying not to get caught and served up on a plate.

'All this time,' Ashley said, her breathing growing quicker.

'What?' Kim asked, confused.

'Tim,' she replied and began to slow down. Kim grabbed her, but Ashley came to a full stop. 'All this time, he was one of those... monsters. All this time.'

'Don't think about that,' Kim ordered, trying to pull her on. She didn't need Ashley breaking down and losing it. She needed her friend to show the fight she had hinted at before.

'But, we were... we've been together,' Ashley said. Kim understood, her own stomach was lurching at the thought of that fiend putting his hands on her friend, so God knew how that made Ashley feel.

But it still wasn't helping.

'You had no way to know what he was,' Kim said, taking deep breaths while she could. Part of her was thankful for the break, but a bigger part of her knew they needed to move. 'Forget it. Be sad when we get out of here.'

'And I said it, Kim. I told him I loved him. He said it too.'

'He's a liar,' Kim snapped, raising her voice as much as she dared and as much as her oxygen-starved body would allow. 'If you want to feel anything, feel anger. Feel angry at who he is and what he did. Use that. Channel it and fucking use it.'

'But—'

'But nothing. He used you, Ashley. He walked all over you. So what are you going to do about it?'

Ashley didn't say anything, she began to sob. Maybe giving her a hug would have helped calm her down, but Kim didn't have time for that. She needed to snap her friend out of it, and quick. With an open palm, she slapped Ashley hard across the face.

Ashley's eyes popped open in shock, and she instinctively brought a hand up to her cheek.

'What—'

'Enough,' Kim said, cutting in, not letting Ashley even start. 'No more wallowing. No more letting shit just happen to you, Ashley. You need to start fighting back. And, fuck me, there is no better time to start than right now. Because if you don't, honey, we die. Do you want to die?'

'No,' Ashley said, 'of course not.' The words still sounded too timid for Kim's liking, so she shoved her friend, hard, pushing her a few steps back.

'What they hell is wrong with you?' Ashley asked with a hint of anger. But only a hint.

'What's wrong with *me*?' Kim asked, shaking her head. 'I want to get out of this alive, Ashley. And I know we need to fight our way out if we are going to do that. You still sound like you're waiting for someone to come along and save us.

Newsflash, that isn't going to happen. We save ourselves or we die. Understand?'

'Yes,' Ashley said, but again, far too timidly.

'Then mean it,' Kim said and pushed her again.

'Stop it,' Ashley said, clenching her jaw. 'We don't have time for this.'

'Make me,' Kim said and pushed again. Finally, Ashley broke. Kim was taken by surprise as Ashley suddenly stepped forward and pushed her in return, with force, causing Kim to topple backwards onto her backside. It wasn't enough to hurt, but the strength of her friend shocked her.

Good.

'Kim,' Ashley said, bringing a hand up to her mouth, 'I'm—'

'No,' Kim said, quickly getting to her feet. 'No, you're not sorry. You were standing up for yourself. Don't be sorry. Just stay angry. Do you understand what I'm trying to tell you?'

Ashley let her hand fall from her mouth and took a moment. Her jaw set and she tilted her head up and nodded.

'Yes,' she said, finally sounding like she meant it.

'Good,' Kim said and put a hand on her taller friend's shoulder. 'So, what do we do now?'

'We get the fuck out of here.'

'Atta girl,' Kim said with a smile.

They both set off running again, and within a few minutes they saw something that gave Kim hope. Ashley had been right to bring them this way.

The trail was up ahead.

'There it is,' Kim said, keeping her voice low.

'I see it,' Ashley confirmed, and they continued running until they set foot onto the dirt track.

'Which way?' Kim asked.

'Right,' Ashley said, 'that should lead us out.'

As suggested, they ran to the right, with Ashley pushing up ahead and Kim, not quite able to keep pace, bringing up the rear.

Again, Kim's legs began to burn and the pain in her chest and side returned. She found herself losing ground on Ashley, who was keeping a steady pace, pumping her arms and legs with quick, even movements. Kim wished she'd spent more time exercising. She had a natural figure that she never had to work at, whereas Ashley, as self-conscious as she was, worked out all the time. That fitness was now helping her friend, while Kim was struggling.

Fuck it, Kim thought, *if I survive this I'm joining a gym.*

On and on they went. Kim's breathing became loud and erratic and she wanted to throw up. But she knew stopping was dangerous, so she pushed herself harder. They broke through into a clearing, giving them a little more visibility, and Kim finally pulled up, unable to go any farther.

'Ashley,' she said with a gasp.

Ashley stopped and turned back. She was red in the face and covered in sweat, but looked like she could easily keep going. 'You okay?' she asked.

Kim nodded, sucking in air. 'Yeah, I just need to get my breath. Feel like I'm going to pass out.'

Ashley nodded. 'Be quick,' she said.

'I will.' Kim bent over and rested her hands on her knees, trying to stop her head from spinning. Her breathing was quick, too quick.

'Take slow, deep breaths,' Ashley said. 'It'll help.'

Kim closed her eyes and tried to do just that, though it was difficult. Her natural reaction was to pull in as much air to her lungs as she could, but soon she managed to steady her breathing and things began to settle down. The dizziness dissipated and the fire that burned through her muscles and chest eased, if only a little.

Finally, she stood back up to full height. Time to get going again.

Kim had no idea how long it had been since they had left the family behind, but she knew the two lunatics would be closing in.

The hunt was on.

That thought in itself gave Kim another burst of adrenaline. 'Okay,' she said, 'time to go.'

But when she looked over at her friend, she saw a troubled look on Ashley's face.

'What is it?' Kim asked.

'I recognise this place.'

'You mean we've passed through here?'

Ashley nodded. 'Yeah.'

'That's good, it means we are on the right track.'

Kim looked around as well, trying to see if she recognised her surroundings, but not expecting to glean much. To her, one tree looked just like another, especially in the dark. Nothing seemed familiar, so she turned back to her friend, just in time to see her face drop. Ashley held up the torch and pointed it off to their side, and Kim followed the beam of light.

Now she realised exactly where they were.

She saw that flap of skin, the yawning face, still hanging from the tree branch.

They were at the site where they'd found the faceless man.

The one Tim had killed by crushing his skull.

An act that now, knowing what they knew, would probably fit Tim's character very well.

'Okay,' Kim said, 'at least we know we're definitely on the right track. Let's keep moving.'

Seeing the mask of skin again was still disturbing, but there was no need to stop on account of it anymore. They knew who it had belonged to and, likely, the reason for its removal. It should have been of no further concern to them.

'Wait,' Ashley said, moving her beam around. 'Don't you see?'

'See what?' Kim asked as Ashley's beam settled on a spot on the ground up ahead. There was nothing of any real interest, just more of the forest floor.

But then Kim saw the stain; smears of blood.

'The man,' Ashley said. 'He's gone.'

19

Ted kept low as he ran, sweeping over the ground in quick strides. His dull, dirty blade was already drawn, ready to cut and cleave.

Excitement consumed him.

Before, he had simply been their tracker, watching his brother lead the group back to the house. Now, his role was different, one he enjoyed so much more.

Now he was the hunter.

He and his twin sister, Claudia, would have no problem tracking down these two feeble girls. The only question would be how quickly they would do it.

To find them, he knew he had to think like them, and scared people were disappointingly predictable people. They would return to the thing they knew, the thing that would give them the best chance of getting free.

To reach the house, they'd followed the old trail his family had deliberately carved years ago, which meant they would try to find it again and follow it out.

That meant he and his sister just had to do the same thing, only quicker, to catch up to them.

Disappointingly easy.

Still, they made sure to keep off the trail and stick to the trees, weaving between them silently. If they were on the trail and the girls looked back, they would be seen. Not that it really mattered, their prey would still be caught, but sticking to the shadows allowed them to attack when they were ready, and that would make the capture quick and simple.

His sister, Claudia, had dropped the torch she had been carrying as soon as they'd set off in chase, and they were both keeping pace with each other, pushing each other on.

'Been such a long time since we've done this, brother,' she said to him quietly. He didn't need to worry about her talking too loudly; they hadn't made up enough ground just yet for the two little rabbits to hear them.

'Too long,' Ted replied.

'Family's been getting anxious. Fighting all the time.'

'That happens the longer we wait.'

'Stupid, though. Pointless.'

'It is, sister. But we can't help it.'

'Can't control it.'

'No, we can't. It will always rise to the surface. Unless we feed it.'

'Ever wonder what would happen if we didn't feed it? Just let it take over?'

'No, sister.'

'I have. I'd imagine we would end up trying to rip each other to little pieces. Small enough to gobble down.'

'You might be right. It controls and consumes us. That's just the way of things. But we won't let it get that far. Never have before, never will.'

'I dunno,' his sister said. 'Sounds like fun. Henry could feed us all for eternity.'

He laughed, louder than he intended, and he quickly admonished himself.

Stop playing around. Stick to the hunt.

'You might be right, but Henry would take some effort putting down.'

'We could do it,' his sister said. 'Together.'

'Thought about it, have you?'

'A few times. When things get boring around here, the mind wanders.'

'Well, the mind has something to concentrate on now.'

'The hunt.'

'Yes, sister,' he said. 'The hunt.'

She giggled excitedly. It was a sweet sound to him, one that spurred him on. He could almost taste both of the little rabbits that hopped on ahead. He tried to imagine the flavour of the redhead.

He even considered having a little taste before getting them back home.

His stomach churned in anticipation.

Soon it would be time to feast.

20

STILL SLUNG OVER Henry's shoulder, Craig was taken back down the steps to the basement. He half expected the creaking stairs to give way, but they held, clearly made of stronger stuff than they originally seemed. Henry then walked between the hanging bodies, allowing Craig to see their withered, skeletal faces, and smell their awful stench, as he was carried onwards to the far wall.

There was a thick, strong-looking wooden door set into the wall, which Henry pushed open, revealing a corridor behind. The walls of the corridor were nothing more than dirt, tunnelled into the ground, held back by timber strutting. Small, electrical lights hung from the struts, giving a small amount of illumination to the corridor.

Cold air rolled over Craig, as well as a musty, earthy odour.

A little farther ahead, stone steps dropped sharply down. Henry continued down the steps, eventually coming to an open area.

Like the tunnel before, this room seemed to have been carved out of the earth that surrounded it. He could see the underside of the basement floor high above him, held up by stone pillars. Electrical lanterns were fixed to the walls, lighting the room in a dull glow. Maybe the house had a generator?

Situated in the centre of the room, and clearly the focal point, was a large, stone table. Its surface was stained with a dirty brown substance—Craig knew exactly what that was —and there were small holes lining its surface.

Just to the right of that, a side table stood empty, as if waiting to take something on it. An old crate sat in one corner of the room and, at the back, set into the floor, was a metal grate. Behind that, against the far wall, there was what Craig assumed to be some kind of honest-to-God occult fucking altar.

On top of the macabre shrine, with carvings of monstrous, twisted things, there was a human skull, surrounded by smaller skulls; those of animals and, dear God, children. The flat section of the altar held a thick, yellowed book, which stood upright on a perch. It was open and, on its yellowed pages, Craig could make out scribbled writings and sketches, though they were too far away to see clearly.

Was that what all this was? Were these people some kind of cultists?

Did anyone really believe things like that in the modern age?

Unfortunately for Craig, it seemed that some people still did. It may have been backwards and idiotic, but that still didn't help Craig in his current situation.

Henry walked towards the large stone table and dropped Craig roughly onto it. Craig squealed in pain, but Henry just laughed, clearly amused.

Craig was then de-clothed, leaving him completely

naked, and his body was forcibly straightened out. He felt another crunch in his spine, and his legs went completely numb. He continued to scream, feeling more mind-shattering pain than he could take.

The hulking man-child looked down at him.

'Almost done,' Henry said, smiling. 'Just going to need to tie you up.'

'Please,' Craig managed to whisper out. 'I'm begging you.'

'Yeah,' Henry said, 'you are. But the begging is going to get a whole lot worse, I think.'

Henry then got to work, pulling great chains across Craig's body, chains that looped through metal rungs around the table's perimeter. While the monster worked, Craig took further note of the small, circular holes in the stone, holes that were roughly the size of a penny. The only purpose he could see for them was to drain fluid from the table's surface.

Which meant things were going to get messy.

Once Henry had finished restraining Craig, he leaned in close, so that Craig could smell his rotten breath.

'Just one little taste,' Henry whispered, salivating. Craig then screamed as Henry's stubby teeth sank into his shoulder. They cut through his flesh and pulled away, tearing away skin and meat as they did.

Henry sighed contentedly as he chewed. The monster then waved with a blood-stained smile, turned, and left. The sound of his booming footsteps soon grew distant, leaving Craig in terrible pain.

All alone.

Just waiting to die.

He wept.

21

'HOW CAN HE BE GONE?' Kim asked. 'He was dead. We saw it.'

That was the question troubling Ashley. 'Maybe there are more of them out here. Maybe they took him?' Ashley whispered.

'Shit,' Kim said. 'Remember what Tim said, that there was, what, eight of them? Does that mean there could be more running around out here?'

It certainly seemed that way to Ashley. She looked around, letting the beam from her torch penetrate the darkness, fully expecting to see something hiding in the black.

She found nothing.

She reached into her pocket and pulled out her phone, checking the signal.

Nothing.

She'd been making a habit of checking it since the shit had hit the fan, but this place was a dead zone.

'Okay,' Ashley said, 'this doesn't change anything.'

'I agree,' Kim said, putting away her phone. 'We still need to move, regardless.'

Just as they were about to run, Ashley heard something.

The squeak of a small animal. Ashley wasn't an expert by any stretch, but it didn't seem like the normal noise of everyday animal life. It sounded somehow distressed. Before she could ignore it out of hand, she heard it again.

'What is that?' Kim asked.

They heard a wet, sloppy, crunching sound as the squeaks were cut off. The noise had come from a tree up ahead, one with a thick trunk that Ashley recognised. The trail they were on led up past it, but not too close.

'Doesn't matter,' Ashley whispered, not wanting to investigate. 'We just keep going.'

Kim nodded her agreement and they set off again, slowly this time. The wet noise, which Ashley realised was some kind of chewing, persisted.

Something was feeding.

Her hope was that it was just an animal eating another, less-fortunate creature. Things like that happened in the wild, it was the natural order of things, so as long as the predator showed no interest in them, then hopefully they could just carry on.

It had occurred to Ashley that, as little noise as they were making whilst moving, most animals had highly tuned hearing and would probably have heard their footsteps no matter how quiet they tried to be.

Which meant that whatever was currently feasting didn't care enough about them to stop.

Ashley kept her eyes on the tree as she moved, careful not to shine her light on it directly for fear of drawing attention. They slowly circled the wide trunk, making as little noise as possible, and Ashley braced herself for what she would see.

It was dark, but she could just make something out, sitting against the base of the tree.

It was no animal.

It was distinctly human.

'What is it?' Kim whispered, evidently looking as well.

Ashley couldn't help herself, she slowly brought her flashlight up, needing to see what, or who, it was.

What she saw wasn't possible.

Couldn't be.

Kim let out a gasp. It was her noise, rather than the light from the flashlight, that drew the thing's attention.

The thing that should be dead.

The faceless man.

It was an impossibility, but there he was, sitting against the tree, gnawing on what appeared to be a half-eaten squirrel. Half of the animal's chewed body hung from the man's chomping mouth as he looked over in their direction, alerted by Kim's gasp.

Slowly, he got to his feet, and half of the mangled squirrel fell to the floor.

Ashley wanted to scream, but suppressed the urge. There was something slightly different about the man now. When they had found him earlier, seemingly dead on the floor, they could clearly see his skull on display, covered by a smattering of flesh. Now, however, the meat had somehow grown thicker, covering the bone beneath completely.

And that made about as much sense as him still being alive after what Tim had done to him. And yet, Ashley's eyes were not deceiving her. Kim was seeing exactly the same thing.

'That's impossible,' her friend whispered. Ashley had to agree, but they were seeing the impossible. The man began walking towards them, and Ashley put a hand on Kim's shoulder and tugged.

'Let's go,' she said, wanting to be free of these woods now more than ever.

What the hell was he? How was his flesh growing back like that?

No one could survive what he'd been through, let alone be up and walking around already.

The girls turned and began to run, making more noise, but not caring. They just needed to get away from him. Their movement seemed to excite the man, and he made a high-pitched noise, something like a giggle, and ran forward himself. However, regardless of the red flesh that had grown back, it was clear to Ashley his eyes had not yet regenerated, and he tripped and stumbled to the ground.

He let out an agitated roar into the night sky, but Ashley and Kim just ran, as fast as they could, away from him. Again and again he yelled as they left him behind.

Something clicked in Ashley's mind as she remembered how this grotesque man had attacked them earlier. What they had mistaken for fear and instinct was, in fact, aggression. It was clear to her that he wasn't friendly, and never had been. This man, she knew, somehow belonged to the demented clan that took residence in these woods.

The same family Tim had told them about. But it wasn't an urban legend at all, it was his life, and Tim was one of them.

Part of the Webb family.

Her mind ran back to Tim's story. What else had he said about them? That they served something, something greater than them, something that gave them... what was the word? Power? Abilities?

Could that be the reason the faceless man was able to live, despite all that had been done to him? His screams continued to echo into the night.

'He's pissed,' Kim said, panting. Ashley was about to agree when a thought struck her. Maybe he wasn't angry at all, maybe he was calling out to someone.

Alerting them.

'We need to speed up,' Ashley said.

'What is it?' Kim asked, casting a look around as they raced along the trail.

'I think he's calling to them, the others.'

'Calling to them?'

'His family,' Ashley said. 'Don't you see, Kim? He's one of them.'

It took a moment to make sense to Kim. 'Holy shit,' she eventually said.

'And he's letting them know where we are.'

They both gave an extra burst of speed, reaching down inside for the extra energy, to that place in all of us reserved only for the most desperate of times. Trees flew by quickly as they sprinted. Now that they were on the relatively level footing of the dirt track, they were progressing much quicker than before. The beam of the flashlight bounced manically as they ran, shaking this way and that. Ashley tried to keep it steady as best she could, but seeing what was up ahead was secondary to moving quickly.

'Do you think they're close?' Kim asked between breaths.

'Maybe,' Ashley said. 'If they heard our friend back there, then they won't be far behind.'

'Fuck.'

'But that just means we need to be quicker than them.'

'Agreed,' Kim said, then added, 'How far until you think we're out of the woods?'

Out of the woods?

That idiom had taken on a very literal meaning to them both. 'I don't know,' Ashley said. 'Hopefully not long.'

'Good,' Kim said, practically wheezing, 'because I'm not sure how much longer I can keep this up.'

'You have to,' Ashley said. 'You told me we needed to fight. Well, this is part of it. You need to push.'

'I'm trying,' Kim said, but she now sounded desperate. Her panting was erratic and heavy, like someone having an asthma attack. It was clear she couldn't go on much longer, not enough to get clear of the woods, but if they stopped, that would only allow the things chasing them to get even closer. Ashley had a feeling those things wouldn't need to stop to catch their breaths, either.

Ashley was also aware that if Kim kept pushing, eventually she would hit a point where she could go no farther, and just collapse.

Then what?

Was Ashley supposed to leave another friend behind?

No, that wasn't an option. She would be damned before she did that. Ashley slowed to a stop, and Kim followed suit, instantly dropping to her knees. The girl laid her hands flat on the dirt and began to dry heave.

Then she vomited.

'It's okay,' Ashley said, rubbing her back. She watched the trees behind them whilst comforting her friend, concentrating for movement in the shadows. Her friend clearly needed time, but they also needed to get moving again, and quickly. Kim heaved a few more times before finally beginning to settle.

'Better?' Ashley asked. Kim just nodded in response, spitting saliva to the floor. 'Okay,' Ashley went on, 'then we need to move again.'

Kim groaned in protest, but got to her feet. Ashley could see her friend's complexion had paled considerably, and she was drenched with sweat. Ashley considered the idea of shedding layers in order to keep their body temperature down as they ran, but knew they would need their coats and packs if they got clear of the woods. It was still a hell of a hike back through the wilderness, out in the open, where the temperature would drop even further. Chances were, these things would follow them for as long as they could, for as far as they could, but that was something they would just have to deal with. Maybe they would have a better chance of survival out in the open.

Just as they were about to set off again, Ashley realised that the faceless man's howling had ceased.

'He's gone quiet,' she said.

'Why?' Kim asked, still panting.

'I don't know. Either he's just given up, or...'

'Or he's alerted whoever he needed to.'

That meant the two Webb's that were chasing them had made up a hell of a lot of ground. If they were that quick in closing the gap, what chance did the two of them have to make it out?

Not much.

Ashley clenched her jaw. Some hope, no matter how small, was better than none. And until she had breathed her last, she resolved that she wouldn't give up, that she would keep on trying.

Kim was right, they needed to fight. No matter what.

She grabbed her friend, pulled her forward again, and broke into a run, but Kim quickly fell behind.

'This is killing me,' she said.

'No,' Ashley replied, 'this isn't killing you. But if we stop, then the people chasing us will.'

'Okay,' Kim said, 'I get it. I'm fine. Let's keep going.'

Despite her words to the contrary, Ashley didn't know how much more Kim had left.

22

TED AND CLAUDIA had followed the trail from the shadows, amongst the trees, right up to the first clearing from the house. In past hunts their prey often stopped there, the thinking being that the small, open area would give them a better chance of seeing their pursuers coming. That might have been the case, but it never made a difference. More often than not, it ended up being the place of their final stand.

So, Ted was a little surprised to find the two girls hadn't stopped here. Surprised, and, if he was honest, relieved. He didn't want the chase to be over just yet.

He was having far too much fun.

However, though the girls weren't here, he and his sister did find someone else. The voice that called to them was unclear and incoherent, but it was Claudia who had recognised it first.

'That's David,' she'd said.

Upon reaching the clearing, Ted found that she was right.

Their older brother was sitting in the clearing, on the

dirt floor, screaming up at the moon like a baying wolf. Ted could see that he was still missing his face, though things had slowly started to reform. However, the gory hole in the back of his head would take some healing.

He looked pathetic.

Ted couldn't help but snort a laugh.

'David?' Claudia asked as they approached. The blind man turned, his head following the sound. 'Everyone's been looking for you.'

'And what the hell happened to your face? Did Henry do that to you? You must've really pissed him off.'

David got to his feet, grunting angrily, but unable to talk.

'It looks like it hurts like a mother fucker,' Ted said with a chuckle. 'What the hell did you do to piss him off so much?'

'Think his jaw is out of its socket,' Claudia said. 'That'll take a bit to heal up,'

'So will the hole in his head. And his face,' Ted replied. 'Still, he never was a looker. This might be an improvement.'

David clenched his fists and started to stomp over to them.

'Oh,' Ted said, 'I think he's angry.'

'I think he just might be,' his sister agreed. 'Come on, David, what are you really gonna do to us like that?'

David drew closer and began swinging his fists in wide arcs, though they weren't close to hitting either of them. Claudia quickly sidestepped one of his swings and, in one fluid motion, pulled out her gleaming knife and plunged it into David's gut. He moaned in pain and sunk to a knee. Claudia then, shrieking with laughter, pulled the blade upwards as hard she could, opening him up.

David's intestines bubbled out from his stomach and, despite trying to catch them and push them back, slipped through his hands like wet, red spaghetti. His insides spilled to the dirt floor, and David slumped forward on top of them, his impact giving off a loud squelch.

Ted doubled over in laughter. 'Man, I almost feel sorry for you. You've had one shitty day, brother. If you don't get your shit together, you might not even make the feast tonight.'

David just moaned from his position, face down, on the ground.

'Ah, that'd be a shame,' Claudia said, kicking him in the head. Ted saw something grey dislodge and roll from the opening. 'Guess we'll have to take his share.'

'Not a bad plan, sis,' Ted said. 'Speaking of which, I think we should stop fucking about here and go get us our dinner. What do ya' say?'

Claudia smiled and licked the smear of blood from her knife. 'I think that's a fine idea, brother. But you gotta try and keep up.'

They both set off at full sprint, leaving their other brother behind.

23

KIM FELT like she was dying.

The exhaustion her body was enduring was at an intensity she'd never experienced. She had never run this fast, for this long, in her life, and her lungs felt like they would give up the ghost at any minute.

Her lack of physical fitness had already slowed their progress twice, forcing them to stop so she could recover. After all her talk of fighting through what lay ahead and not giving up, it looked like she was going to be undone by nothing more than physical exertion.

Yet Ashley ploughed on, unwavering, like a machine.

So, Kim forced herself to keep going, to dig deeper. She couldn't be the reason they were caught.

She had been given a great incentive when they'd both heard a horrible belly laugh in the distance. Their pursuers weren't far behind.

That spurred her on a little, and the extra adrenaline helped her fight through the pain, despite every deep, wheezing breath feeling like she was drawing fire into her lungs.

The trail then started up a gentle incline, causing her legs and muscles to strain in protest. Then, to top it off, she felt a sudden, severe pain erupt in her calf, almost like she had been stabbed.

'Ow,' she said, reducing her run to a hop. Then she realised what it was; she hadn't been stabbed, it was simply a cramp. She could feel her calf knotting up, causing the sharp sting to trickle out through her muscle.

'What happened?' Ashley asked as she stopped and turned around. Kim set off again, trying to ignore the pain. It was more of a shuffle and a hop than a run.

'Just a cramp,' she said, 'keep going.'

And they did, but it took Kim a while to get into full flow again and, even when the worst of the cramp finally abated, her leg still felt sore as hell. Every footfall was painful.

'Keep going,' Ashley called back to her, encouraging her on.

She was about to answer and assure her friend she had no intention of stopping, when something to her left caught her eye.

Some kind of movement, from deep within the trees. Instinctively, she flashed her torch over in that direction, hoping to see what it was. It seemed the movement also caught Ashley's attention as well, and she, too, pointed her beam in the same direction.

'What is it?' she asked.

'I thought I saw something,' Kim replied.

Then their beams picked up what it was, illuminating it fully, and Kim's blood ran cold.

It was the thin man, the one who had been chasing them.

The one known as Ted.

He moved through the trees with such speed and fluidity it was scary. And the fact he could do so without looking ahead, only looking directly at them like a wolf eyeing its prey, unnerved her even more. His giddy, deranged smile was almost enough to tip her over the edge.

Realising he had been seen, the man's response was to simply laugh.

'Run,' Kim screamed, and Ashley sped up.

'Fuck, fuck, fuck,' Ashley said again and again, panic in her voice.

'Found em, sis,' the man shouted. 'Time to take em down.'

He laughed again, a high-pitched cackle.

Fuck, fuck, fuck.

Kim couldn't see the girl he was talking to, despite flicking her torch around. She would have expected his sister to be close to him, but could see nothing.

Too late, Kim realised where she was.

'On it,' she heard a female voice say from the other side of the trail. A blur of movement sprung from those trees ahead and crashed into Ashley.

Kim heard her friend yell in shock. Ashley was lifted from her feet and thrown to the ground by the girl, who fell on top of her, cackling like an excited witch.

In that instant, Kim knew she had a choice to make. An idea popped into her head, one she wasn't proud of.

While Ashley struggled with the wild woman, who began punching and striking, Kim saw an opportunity. If she were to keep going, then maybe both of the pursuers would focus on Ashley, giving her chance to escape. It was a shameful thought, and worse, one that was realised as Kim continued on past her friend.

'Kim,' Ashley yelled. After a few strides, Kim stopped and turned back.

What the hell am I doing?

The wild woman had pinned Ashley's arms to her sides, and Ashley looked over to Kim with unbelieving, pleading eyes, astounded that her friend was about to abandon her.

'I'm sorry,' Kim said, still not certain of what she would do. Was this an apology for a past action, or for one yet to come?

As it turned out, she didn't get the chance to decide. The man leapt from the trees, shoulder first, and knocked Kim painfully to the floor. She cried out as the torch slipped from her grasp and rolled away. She felt the man's heavy weight drop onto her and could smell his putrid, sour stench.

'Made that easy for us,' he said as he overpowered her. 'One day, one of you people will give us a good hunt.'

Kim writhed and fought, trying to pull her arms free to lash out, but it was no good, she was completely outmatched. The man held something up, just below her chin, and Kim felt a hard, cold point press into her skin.

She knew what it was.

The blade then moved lower and angled itself to lie across her throat. The man raised his eyebrows in expectation. Kim understood the order and fully believed he would carry out his implied threat and slice open her throat, so she stopped her struggling.

Keeping the long knife in place, the man unraveled something from around his waist with his free hand. He held up a length of rope.

'Fucking bitch,' Kim heard. The voice was that of the woman wrestling with Ashley, who still hadn't given up. Looking over, Kim saw the girl was holding her nose, which was dripping with blood. Some of it had smeared on Ashley's forehead.

Had Ashley head-butted her?

'Having trouble, sis?' the man called over, his tone more amused than concerned.

'I got it,' the girl snapped angrily. She then began punching Ashley, again and again, and clawing at her face. 'You keep still or I'll claw your fucking eyes out!'

But Ashley didn't listen.

The man sighed and pressed the blade harder against Kim's throat, drawing her attention back to him. 'You,' he said, 'be good. And roll over.'

He moved off her and turned Kim over himself, not giving her a chance to disobey. She then felt him go to work, wrapping her hands tightly together as her face was pressed into the ground. Once her hands were secured, the length of rope was pulled down, and her legs pulled up. Soon, she was completely hog-tied. Then the man got to his feet and walked over to help his sister, who was still struggling with Ashley.

Ashley's face was heavily bloodied, but that didn't seem to slow her. Hell, given the way she was fighting, Kim thought she might just have a chance at escape, if it weren't for the man walking over to aid his sister, doubling the odds against Ashley.

Together, the siblings were able to completely overpower her, roll her over, and tie her up the same as Kim. When they were done, the young woman let loose with a fierce kick to Ashley's ribs.

'Some fight in this one,' the man said, looking down at Ashley. 'Gotta say, that's a surprise. I heard them call her the mouse and thought she would be the easiest to break.'

The woman held her nose, which was still dribbling

blood. 'She will fucking break. I'm gonna see to that. Bitch fucked my nose.'

She kicked Ashley again, who let out a groan.

As the woman lashed out at her, Ashley never once looked up to her captors, she just stared angrily back at Kim. Despite being terrified for her life, Kim couldn't help but feel absolutely ashamed with herself.

Would she really have left her friend, given the chance? They'd both abandoned Craig quickly enough. Would she have done the same thing again, had she not been stopped?

It was a question she didn't know the answer to.

The man approached her again. 'Right, little girl, time to get going. We have somewhere to be. You and your friend are the guests of honour.'

He reached down and heaved her up, first pulling her to sitting position, then lifting her up onto his shoulder. Kim heard him strain a little, but his hold seemed strong. She found herself looking down the length of his back, where she could see his knobbly spine poke through the thin, dirty cotton of his tank top. She could also see that, under the top, his skin was littered with small, weeping sores. It was a disgusting sight, but rather that than having to face Ashley's accusing eyes.

'Can you carry that one, sis?' the man asked. 'Or do you wanna take mine? She's a bit smaller?'

'I got her,' the woman called back angrily. Kim heard her strain and heave. 'See,' the girl said, her voice shaking with exertion.

'Don't look like you got her,' the man said. 'Here, let's swap.'

'I said I got it,' the girl snapped. 'Now come on, let's go.'

'If you say so,' the man said, and they began walking.

Kim knew they were on their way back to the house,

back to that horrible family, and she knew they would end up like all those other people who hung from the ceiling of the basement: desecrated, feasted upon, and quite dead. The thought of her body hanging there, in that room, as her final resting place, was terrifying. She would be forever trapped in that place of evil, and her family would never know what had become of her.

Though maybe that was a good thing.

Regardless, Kim began to weep.

The man carrying her heard her sobs and began to chuckle. 'There, there,' he whispered. 'I know it's scary. But try to look on the bright side. You get to see your friend again, back at the house. You know, the one you left behind. The family will have him ready by now and he'll be waiting for you. I'm sure he's eager to see you both again. Isn't that nice?'

'Let me go,' Kim whispered.

'And when we're back,' he went on, ignoring her, 'and you see your friend again, and you're all reunited as one happy family, you two girls get to watch. You get to watch as we eat him. As we cut him up while he's still alive and squirming. Fair warning though, the family all have big appetites, so it tends to get a little... messy.'

'Please,' Kim pleaded, but still he ignored her.

'And then,' he said, 'then it'll be your turn. We'll strap you down and decide which piece of you we want to cut off first. It'll hurt, and you'll be helpless to do anything, only watch as we start to eat you alive. Oh, and I think Henry has a bit a soft spot for you as well, so he might want first go. You have nice eyes, you see, and that's Henry's thing. He finds eyes delicious. I'm not much of a fan, myself, they're surprisingly hard, and the juice from them when they pop doesn't have much flavour. So, I'll let my little brother have them. I'm more of a leg man, myself.'

It was all too much. His cruel description of the events to come finally pushed Kim over the edge.

She began to scream hysterically.

The man just laughed, clearly pleased with himself.

24

Craig's shoulder still ran with blood and felt like it was on fire. He kept looking at the open wound, at the chunk of flesh that had been taken from him.

A small taste of what was to come.

He could see the exposed shoulder bone poking through the wet meat, and the pain of the wound, coupled with that of his back and ribs, was unbearable. There was no way to find even a moment's respite from its constant torment.

He heard footsteps return. Not just the heavy stomps of Henry, but others too. And voices as well, murmurs, that increased in volume the closer they got, until the family revealed themselves to him once again.

The man with the beard was first, followed by the woman Craig presumed was his wife, then Tim, who had changed from his hiking gear into dirtied jeans and a loose shirt, and finally Henry. The large freak pushed his bulbous frame through the door opening.

Tim waved at Craig. 'How you doing?'

'Tim,' Craig begged, 'please help.'

Tim just laughed, then ignored him and turned back to

the others. 'You know,' he said to them, 'Ted and Claudia won't be happy with us starting without them. Neither will David.'

'Well,' the older man said, 'Ted and Claudia should have been back by now. They'll probably be fucking around with the two girls anyway, so let them have their fun. Besides, there'll be plenty to go around. After first helping we can go and fetch David, make sure he gets something too.'

'He can have the scraps,' Tim said. 'I eat properly this time, Da, you promised.'

Craig noticed the man and woman give each other a look. The man's brows knitted into a frown. 'Look, son,' he said, 'you can't have too much.'

'But you said,' Tim shouted suddenly, like an indignant child.

'We need you how you are, Tim. You know that,' the mother said.

'You'll still get to eat,' the man added. 'But we can't give you too much. We can't have you going through any kind of change. We need you how you are.'

'I'm sick of this,' Tim yelled, throwing his hands up in the air. 'It's always *next time*, always another excuse. I'm sick of it, sick of being the runt. I want what I'm owed.'

'In time,' the mother said. 'But we can't feed if we don't have people to feed on.'

'Exactly,' the father agreed. 'It's not like any of us can get people back here, looking like we do. We don't blend in. You still do. We need that.'

'But then I'll never have enough. I'll never get stronger.'

'You will, I promise. But the more you have, the more you crave, and after you have too much, you change. There's no going back from that. We need to keep you at a certain level. Need to make sure we keep things in balance.'

'You're lying,' Tim shouted. Henry chuckled, seemingly amused. 'Fuck you, fatty,' Tim said.

'Runt,' Henry replied, still laughing.

'Please, Timothy,' the mother said. 'We'll figure this out, I promise. But right now, we need you to do what's right for the family.'

'I'm part of this family, too,' Tim said, 'and nothing we do is ever right by me.'

The older man stepped forward and swung his arm, cracking Tim on the side of the face with the back of his hand, knocking Tim backwards a few steps.

'Enough,' the man yelled and struck his son again. 'This is how it has to be. You are part of this family and you will do as you're fucking told.'

'But—'

'But nothing,' the man said. His mouth then formed into a sneer. 'If you won't listen to us, there is another option, you know.'

'What do you mean?'

'If you think you have it so bad, I can take you down *there*. We can go see Grandpa. See what he thinks of all this. What do you say?'

The suggestion sounded exactly like a threat, and after the man said it, Craig saw Tim's face turn white.

'No,' he said, quickly. 'No, not that.'

'You sure?' the man asked, rubbing a hand through his beard. 'That would sure resolve things, don't you think?'

'I'm sure,' Tim said. 'It's just frustrating, Da, that's all. But I know what I gotta do, for the good of the family. I do. And I won't let you down.'

The older man looked at Tim, considering his plea. He finally nodded, pleased with the answer. 'Good,' he said.

'Now let that be the end of it.' He grabbed his son and pulled him into an embrace.

'I'm sorry,' Tim said, his voice muffled by his father's shoulder.

'That's okay,' the man said, stroking Tim's hair. 'Just remember, we're a family, so we gotta do what's right for each other. Always put the family first, that's the most important thing.'

'I will.'

'Good boy,' the man said and released Tim. The bearded man then walked over to Craig and looked down at him. Then he noticed the wound on Craig's shoulder, and his face screwed up in confusion. 'What the fuck is this?' He looked up to Henry, who took a step back, hanging his head like a scolded dog. 'What did you do?'

'I got a little hungry,' the giant said.

'A little hungry? You took a chunk clean out of him.'

'He's on the table,' Henry said, 'so nothing's getting wasted.'

'Did you hear what I just said to your brother? About putting the family first and making sacrifices? Here I am trying to keep things in order, and you can't keep your damn stomach under control for a little while longer. Damn it, Henry.'

'I'm sorry, Da,' Henry said.

'I don't want to hear it,' the man said, holding up a hand. 'You shouldn't have done it, so that means you don't get to eat until Ted and Claudia bring back the next course.'

'What?' Henry asked, incredulous. 'That ain't fair.' His already high-pitched voice went up a few octaves.

'Oh come on now, honey,' the mother said. 'You can't do that to him, it's just cruel.'

'I can,' the man said, defiantly. 'Tim has had to eat scraps all these years and this fat fuck can wait a little longer for his supper.'

'Don't call me that,' Henry said in a whiny voice.

'Benjamin,' the woman said, seemingly appalled. 'How can you say that to him? That's horrible.'

'Don't take his side, woman,' the man said. 'He's like this because he always gets his own way and doesn't know any control.'

'That isn't true,' she argued.

'Then what about David? This big idiot left one of our own all busted up and out in the open.'

'Oh,' she said, 'David will be fine. He's been through worse.'

'That's not the point. These people,' he pointed to Craig, 'found him. If it weren't for Tim, everything could have gone to hell.'

'You're being dramatic,' the woman said, having none of it. Craig always assumed parents weren't supposed to play favourites, but that clearly didn't apply to this woman.

'You're doing it again, Adela. Letting him off the hook.'

'Well someone needs to cut him a little slack,' she spat back. 'You have him chained up in the basement every chance you get, for the littlest things. All he has to do is breathe wrong and you throw him down there. It isn't healthy for a boy.'

Craig's mind was swimming. The whole scene was farcical.

He'd seen his fair share of family disputes, but even the most fucked up ones on national television didn't compare to this. They were talking about what could be considered normal family issues; how to raise and discipline a child, but all of it was borne from the act of... eating people. They were murderers, psychopaths, and cannibals, and here they were bickering about how best to raise a child.

A child that was bigger than any human Craig had ever seen.

If he hadn't been in so much agony, the whole thing would have been funny.

'It's what he needs,' the man said.

'Do I really have to wait?' the hulk asked, looking at his mother with puppy dog eyes.

She walked over and gently rubbed his massive arm. 'Of course you don't, sweetie. Daddy was just upset that you started a little early.'

'Damn it, Adela,' the man yelled.

Overruled, Craig thought.

'Just promise you'll try and control yourself in the future,' she said to him.

'I will, I swear,' Henry said, now smiling.

'Why the hell do I bother?' the father said. 'Fucking waste of time.'

'It's sorted now,' the mother said. 'So stop going on about it.'

'He'll never learn if you keep babying him. Look at him, Adela, he ain't no fucking child. Hell, he ain't even the youngest any more. You don't treat Timothy that way.'

'Timothy knows I love him,' the woman said, still looking up at Henry, still stroking his arm. Craig looked over to Tim, who was scowling. Clearly he wasn't as assured of his mother's love as she thought he was.

The father let out a sigh and shook his head. 'Fine,' he said, 'but he can put himself to use. Henry, go and get the stuff.'

Before obeying the command, the giant looked to his mother first, who smiled and nodded. He then walked over to the corner of the room, to the old wooden crate Craig had noticed earlier. He flipped open the lid and pulled something out. When the monster stood, Craig saw that whatever he was holding was wrapped up in a dirtied bundle of cloth. Henry slammed down the lid of the crate and made his way back over, handing the bundle to his father.

The father then set the bundle down on the small table to the side of Craig and unravelled it.

Craig began to squirm when he saw the glistening, metallic objects reveal themselves. Large knives, cleavers, hammers, and other carving equipment were laid out. There was even a small hand axe, and something Craig had seen on medical programs for prying open rib cages.

The father plucked up a large cleaver and smiled down at Craig.

'So,' he said, licking his lips, 'who wants a leg?'

25

The woman carrying Ashley was struggling.

Even though she seemed amazingly strong for her lithe build, she had been carrying Ashley for quite a distance now, and Ashley could hear her breathing begin to falter. Her steps, too, became wobbly and uneven.

And if she was weakening, did that reveal an opportunity to Ashley?

If it did, she knew she needed to act quickly, because the man carrying Kim was directly behind them and would see everything. As odds went, they were pretty slim, but Ashley would take slim over hopeless.

But, if by some fluke of circumstance she did manage to get free and have a chance at escape, one issue remained.

Kim.

The girl Ashley considered her best friend in life, someone she loved dearly, someone she thought loved her back. The girl who seemed only too eager to leave her behind.

As angry as she was, Ashley wasn't oblivious to the fact,

though, that both her and Kim had done exactly the same thing to Craig less than an hour ago.

It seemed this was a weekend for turning your back on a friend in need.

In some fucked up kind of way, though, perhaps Tim's betrayal hurt Ashley less than what Kim had almost done. This was his plan all along, after all. He hadn't turned on them; he was never one of them. Not really.

But with Kim it was different. Ashley couldn't shake the look Kim had given after she had run by without helping.

It was almost apologetic.

Which, to Ashley, meant Kim had every intention of continuing on, leaving her behind as a distraction to make good her escape. That hurt more, and cut deeper, than anything Tim and his fucked up family could possibly do.

So, the question remained. If, by some small chance, an opportunity to escape presented itself, would she leave Kim behind? God knows she deserved it.

Ashley didn't know the answer to that question, not yet, and decided it pointless debating it. If an opportunity did arise, she would deal with it then.

The woman carrying her began to stumble with almost every other step, and her breathing turned into a wheeze. She was obviously running out of steam.

'You think we should untie their legs and make them walk for us?' Ashley heard the brother call from behind. 'Might be easier that way.'

He certainly didn't sound as out of breath as his sister was. 'No,' she said defiantly. 'I'm fine.'

The pause, and deep breath, between each word, indicated otherwise. Ashley had half an idea; to try and wriggle free, to make things as difficult as possible for the woman, maybe force her to drop Ashley. But then what? Her brother was still bringing up the rear, and Ashley was completely tied up. What could she possibly do other than flop around on the floor like a fish out of water?

The answer came a short while later, when the girl carrying her eventually gave way to exhaustion and stumbled to the floor. The impact was sudden, but Ashley's fall was broken by the woman, who let out a grunt. She wiggled out from beneath Ashley, panting, and kicked out at her, catching her in the ribs.

'Wanna trade?' the brother said, walking over to them both, Kim still slung over his shoulder.

'I said I'm fine,' his sister said.

'You ain't,' he replied. 'And if we need to keep stopping, this is gonna take too long. You know what the family are like, especially Henry. By the time we get back there'll be no good meat left.'

'We still have these two,' the sister said. 'Plenty of good meat on them.'

'True, but why give up any of it? Who knows when we'll have a feast like this again. Food supply has been getting more scarce year on year.'

'I know that. You think I don't know that?'

'Then let's quit fucking about and get a move on. Here, take this one,' he said.

'No,' the woman said, quickly getting to her feet. She moved too quickly, however, and wavered a little as she stood.

'Will you stop being so damn stubborn?'

'I got this,' she yelled back.

'Fine,' her brother replied. 'Then cut her feet loose and make her walk ahead. It'll be quicker that way.'

'And if she tries to escape?'

'Make sure she doesn't. Make sure she won't even think

about it. Tame the fucking mouse, sis, and be quick about it. I ain't hanging around any longer.'

The man strode on past them and, as he did, Ashley locked eyes with Kim. Ashley scowled, letting her friend, or ex-friend, know exactly how she felt. Then her ribs exploded with pain as the sister, who stood above her, planted another kick into her, this one with the toe of her boot.

'Listen here, bitch,' the girl said, kneeling down close to Ashley. She pulled out a short, hooked blade. 'I'm gonna untie your feet, and you're gonna walk along like a good little doggie. Understand?'

Ashley didn't answer, didn't even look at her.

'If you don't,' the woman started, but held off finishing as she brought the blade to Ashley's cheek. She slowly pushed it into the skin, drawing blood. The pain was sharp and Ashley felt the warm trickle of blood run down her face.

'That's just the start,' the woman said. She then quickly yanked the blade down, hard, completely opening up Ashley's cheek. Ashley howled in pain as the knife easily sliced through the skin. She even felt the tip cut across her gum and scrape her molars as it went.

The woman laughed and stood back up. 'Going to have a nice little scar there, little lady. I made sure to cut deep. Looks like I might have gone too deep, though. Fuck, I can see your jaw and teeth through the opening. Maybe I should have kept it going, whaddya think? Made the gash run into your mouth? That would have been a hell of a thing to show off.'

Ashley squirmed and groaned, feeling more blood spill down her face to the floor. It stung horribly. She saw the woman move, bending down to her feet and pulling at the bonds that tied them. She cut through the rope and Ashley's legs came free.

Ashley felt an opportunity brewing, but she would have to take her chance at the right time. Right now, she was too disoriented from the pain that burned through her cheek.

'Get up,' the woman yelled and kicked her again. Ashley slowly complied and stood to her feet. 'Good little mouse,' the woman said and shoved Ashley forward. 'Now, march.'

Again, Ashley complied, walking forward carefully. With her flashlight gone, she was unsure of her footing, even on the relatively level trail. Her face and cheek continued to burn like a line of fire running down her skin, and blood dropped in steady globules from her chin.

The man carrying Kim was farther up ahead, almost lost to the shadows. That was good, but the woman was pushing Ashley on quickly, which meant they would close the gap in short order. If Ashley was going to make an escape, then she needed to try it when she only had one of them to deal with.

And she would need to put the woman down somehow, at least semi-permanently, in order to get free. Ashley had already seen how quickly the girl could move through these woods, and she would have no trouble catching Ashley if it turned into a straight foot race.

Half a plan developed in her mind, and through sheer desperation, Ashley acted on it as quickly as it had formed. She let an ankle roll beneath her, careful not to let her full weight drop, but trying to make the stumble look convincing, even letting out a small cry of pain as she began hopping forward. She bent double and pulled the supposed bad ankle up from the floor, cradling it with tied hands.

'You fucking idiot,' the girl said. 'I ain't carrying your fat arse anymore, so get a move on.'

Ashley took a step forward and pretended to stumble

again, in pain, as if putting pressure on the ankle was unbearable. The girl pushed her again, and Ashley hobbled, then lowered herself to a crouching position and lifted the foot in question off the floor. She continued to moan, making things as convincing as possible.

'My ankle,' Ashley said. 'I can't... I can't put weight on it.'

'You're going to have to,' the woman said.

'I can't,' Ashley replied, starting to cry.

Once again, the blade was at her throat. 'If you don't, I'll just drain you right here, right now, and let you bleed out on the floor.'

Ashley decided to call her bluff, hoping that the woman had no intention of carrying through with her threat. The goal was to get Ashley back to the house, not kill her out here and let her *meat* go to waste.

She just hoped it wasn't a goal they would easily give up on.

Ashley slowly fell backwards to her butt and kept her leg in the air to avoid putting any pressure on it. She knew she had to catch the woman somehow, in some way, and make her feel it.

The woman bent down close to Ashley, fire in her eyes, and held the blade out. 'I'm not fucking joking,' she said.

Ashley saw her chance.

As the woman leaned closer to issue more threats, Ashley pushed her raised foot forward, as hard as she could, driving her heel into the girl's nose with every ounce of power she could muster. Ashley heard a crunch and the girl's head snapped back. She dropped the blade and stumbled backwards a few steps.

Ashley acted quickly, diving for the blade, which she grabbed with her tied hands. She was back on her feet in no time and charged into the woman, shoulder first. The girl fell to the floor and Ashley landed on top of her.

There was a moment where the girl, Claudia, Ashley remembered, looked up in disbelief. Disbelief that this little mouse was able to outwit her and get the upper hand.

Ashley didn't dwell on it; she swiftly raised the knife high above her, grasped in both hands, and drove it down.

She felt the blade sink into the gut of the woman, who let out a cry of pain. Ashley then pulled the weapon sideways, across the woman's belly, slicing her open, allowing blood and ropey entrails to push their way out.

The girl roared in pain and rolled away, clutching her stomach as red liquid spilled through her fingers.

'Fucking bitch,' she spat, blood running from her mouth.

'Sis?' Ashley heard the man call from ahead. During the conflict, he had obviously kept on going, and Ashley couldn't make him out anymore. The woman groaned and gargled in response, but it was quiet, almost muted. She coughed and spat a splash of blood across the ground.

Ashley's mind raced as to what to do next; the woman was down and didn't look to be getting up any time soon, suffering what may have been a fatal wound. Though remembering the faceless man, it might take a little more to put these people down.

Could they even be killed?

Worth a try.

Ashley then clasped the handle of the blade again and thrust it down, letting her full weight drop behind it. She guided the tip into the side of the girl's head and felt herself stop mid drop, suspended as it initially pierced into the skull with a crack, then held. The girl let out a horrible screech and the blade found its way farther in. Ashley pushed down, forcing it in, and twisted and twirled the blade, attempting to mash up the brain beneath.

The woman thrashed and screamed, blood spilling from her cranium and gut, but her movements were weak.

Realising she still needed to get away, Ashley heaved the knife free, which took three tries, and angled the sharp edge along the ropes that tied her wrists together. She then ran it backwards and forwards, trying to get as much leverage as possible with the awkward grip.

'Sis?' she heard the man shout again, louder this time. Ashley cut at the rope, frantically. The knife was soaked in blood and slippery in her hands, but she worked as quickly as she could.

'Hey,' she heard the man yell, and Ashley looked up. She could see him now, up ahead, still carrying Kim, whom he promptly dropped to the floor like a sack.

Come on, she prayed, willing the knife to do its work much, much faster. The man set off in a sprint towards her and she, in turn, swivelled and ran. Ashley tried to keep on cutting as she fled, but it was hard to keep the knife steady.

Looking back over her shoulder, she saw the man move with frightening speed as he closed the distance, keeping low, like an animal finely-tuned to its environment.

'What do you think you're doing, girl?' he yelled.

Come on, come on, come on.

Ashley then felt the rope finally give and fall slack. She wriggled her hands completely free and let the rope fall, keeping a firm grip on the knife, and ran for her life.

But it was no good, he was just too quick, and he closed the gap in mere moments. Ashley knew he would catch up to her in no more than a few seconds. So, instead of letting that happen, she stopped and turned to face him. She also brought the weapon up and held it out before her, letting him see what was waiting.

The man pulled up short a few feet from her.

'Well, did you take that from my sister?' he asked. He turned back to look at the writhing woman on the floor.

'Stay back,' Ashley said, 'or I'll gut you too.'

The man nodded, seemingly impressed. 'Didn't think you had it in you, little mouse. You're full of surprises, ain't ya? And you did indeed gut my sister, but that only means I gotta do the same to you.' He then pulled free his own long machete. 'Here, let me show you.'

Ashley took a step backwards, still training the knife on him as he took a step forward, matching her movements. Running wasn't an option as the man was far too quick, and this time she had no head start to speak of. If she couldn't run, that left only one thing, and it could very well mean her death. But she knew if she didn't try, then she would die anyway. Hell, at least this way might be quicker, and less painful, than what they had planned for her.

Ashley took a deep breath and tried to steady her nerves.

'You know what,' she said, feeling an odd sense of calm take hold. 'I think I want to give it another try myself.'

The man looked surprised, initially, then he threw his head back and let out a hearty belly laugh. 'Damn, little mouse, I really like you. Shame it's gotta end this way. You would have been fun to play with.'

Ashley didn't wait any longer, she lunged forward, blade first, ready to hack and slash as wildly as she could.

After the first swing, Ashley knew her escape attempt was over.

The man dodged under her arm, and when she tried to bring the knife down to his back, he just feinted to the side, effortlessly avoiding her attacks. He then ducked behind her as she overcommitted again, now completely out of her reach. It was helpless, and Ashley braced herself for the inevitable retaliation.

She felt a swift blow to the back of her head.

Spots of light erupted, pinpricking her vision, and dizziness took hold. She felt her body fall, but as she dropped, she was already feeling far removed from reality. Ashley realised she was losing consciousness, and her last sight was the man standing above her, still smiling.

He raised his knife.

Ashley was thankful that the black swallowed her up, stealing her consciousness, grateful she wouldn't feel the pain of her death.

26

THE MAN HELD up his machete, ready to carve up the girl that had tried to escape.

The meek little mouse.

Obviously not so meek anymore.

In a strange kind of way, maybe the weekend had done her good, shown her what she was really capable of. She'd gotten the better of Claudia, leaving his sister howling and writhing. Ted couldn't remember ever seeing that happen before.

This little mouse had a lot of potential.

Shame he had to kill her.

It wasn't like he hadn't warned her, more than once, yet still she disobeyed. In a way, he could respect that, but rules were rules. He'd told her what would happen, and he needed to follow through. His father always said that if you didn't make good on a threat, then you were nothing, and no one would respect you.

In this world, you had to earn everything.

So, she had to die.

He gripped the handle of the machete tighter.

Didn't she?

In all the years he and his family had been killing and feeding, and it had been too many to keep track of, he'd never really seen anyone like her. She'd proven to have a determination and strength he hadn't seen at first. And she was easy enough on the eye. Even the love mark his sister had bestowed upon her only improved things, as far as he was concerned. Battle scars were sexy, something to be proud of.

Plus, he knew Tim was getting tired of being the youngest, the weakest. His brother was desperate for more. Could it be time to recruit again? It was another mouth to feed, of course, but maybe a good-looking girl like this one would draw more meat out for them.

Maybe the reason things were so rough and sparse at the minute was because they had all stagnated. Things between them hadn't changed for a long, long time.

Was it time for the family to grow?

It had been over forty years since Tim had joined, brought home by father, kidnapped after wandering too close to the woods. Maybe it was time for new blood.

But they could barely feed themselves as they were, so was adding another to their ranks sensible?

Maybe she could replace one of the others?

Tim hadn't proven that useful in luring food, especially not recently, so why not swap him out? And wouldn't it be fitting to swap him with someone he brought in?

The choice, however, was not his to make.

Father would have to make that decision. If he agreed, then the girl would go down to see Grandpa.

And if it wasn't to be, at least they still had another warm body for the feast. Maybe the only stupid decision here was to actually kill her.

Ted slid the machete back into the loop on his trousers, his mind made up. His sister was still rolling around on the floor like a wounded puppy.

'Well, sis?' he said and stepped towards her. 'What happened here?'

'Ted, helgh,' the girl mumbled out, drastically slurring her words. Was that supposed to be *help?* Drool ran from her mouth, mixed with blood. Her jaw worked as she tried to speak again, but it simply gnawed at thin air, refusing to work how it should.

'Oh shit,' Ted said, laughing. 'She broke you, sis. You might be full-on retarded now.' He collapsed to the floor in a fit of hysterics. 'Jesus, she fucking done you over. Do you know how long it'll take to heal up from this? Sorry sis, I don't have that kind of time to wait. I'm going to be late getting back as it is.'

He got to his feet. Claudia reached up for her brother from a pool of her own blood. It was an exciting sight to him.

'Ted,' she pleaded again, forcing out the word.

He just shrugged. 'Ma and Da aren't gonna be happy with you when I tell them. Hell, they might even be impressed with our guest here and have her replace you. Take you both down to see Grandpa and see what he has to say.'

Claudia tried to crawl forward, but her motor skills were obviously affected and her hands didn't seem to move where she wanted them to. It was a comical sight, like a little marionette moving around by unpracticed hands.

Ted turned away and began to tie up the redhead again. Completely this time, like he had done with her friend; feet bound to arms. He wouldn't make the same mistake as his sister.

'Ted,' she said again, the words still coming out as little more than mush.

Ted hoisted the girl up to his shoulder. He looked down at his sister one final time. 'Get home as quick as you can, sis. Food won't keep for too long. Might not be anything left. Imagine that? Imagine that hunger being extended for who knows how long, while the rest of us are content, with full bellies.'

He turned and walked away, leaving her behind to moan helplessly to herself.

He walked over to the other bound girl. She looked up at him in total fear. So helpless and afraid.

Like a scared little mouse.

What an interesting turnaround.

'Okay,' Ted said, pulling free his weapon again with his spare hand. 'I don't think I can trust you enough to let you walk ahead. And I can't carry you both, so what I'm going to do is take off your scalp. That's going to hurt. And, to be honest, I'm only doing it for fun. I don't collect them or anything, I haven't even tried it before. Which is probably why I'm going to do it now. You're going to be my first. And when I'm done, I'm going to bury this thing,' he held up the weapon, 'into your skull, as far as it will go. Like your friend here did to my sister. Don't know if you saw that. Shame, would have been nice to get you back to the house. The family might have had half a mind to keep you around, like a pet. Not much of a life, but at least you'd have been alive.'

He bent down and the woman, on cue, began to beg.

'No,' she pleaded. 'Please, I swear, I won't try to get away. Please. I won't cause trouble. We can go back to the house. I'll walk. I won't run. Anything you want. I swear I won't try anything. Please. Please don't kill me.'

Ted studied her expression and knew that she was

broken. A puppet for him to manipulate. He pretended to give some consideration, before finally giving a nonchalant shrug.

'Fuck it,' he said, 'we'll give it a try. It's not like you'd get far, anyway.'

With his spare hand, he cut free her legs, leaving enough rope loose from her existing bonds for him to hold like a leash. He got to his feet and yanked hard at the rope, forcing the girl up to a standing position.

'Okay, doggie, walk. Follow the trail.'

She did as instructed, walking forward with her head bowed down.

He smiled, pleased with his work.

Despite Claudia's fuck up, he would single-handedly bring both of them back to the family.

And, who knows, maybe even introduce them all to the newest member.

27

CRAIG MANAGED TO SCREAM, even though every movement, no matter how slight, caused him great pain.

'No,' he pleaded as the cleaver was held aloft. 'Please, don't do this, just don't—'

His words turned into a prolonged screech as the father dropped the cleaver, sinking it into the flesh of his thigh. Through it all, he heard the people gathered around him laugh manically.

'I like it when the animals squeal when we slice them up,' the father said. He waggled the knife free and brought it up again. 'Proves you ain't nothing more than a pig. And this leg of yours looks might tasty.'

The cleaver came down again, sinking farther into Craig's thigh. Warm blood squirted free. The pain was white hot.

'Hit a good vein there,' the woman said. 'Careful not to waste any, dear.'

'I won't,' the man said. 'Table's big enough to catch all the blood. Grandpa will get his fill, don't worry.'

Again and again he brought the cleaver down, each time

cutting farther and farther into Craig's leg as the blonde man screamed in agony and desperation. Another chop brought a new, more tender kind of pain as blade met bone.

It was more difficult for the man to shake the blade free this time, and each twist of the metal sent a fiery jolt of agony up the length of Craig's thigh.

Chop, chop, chop.

Through the bone, again into the meat, and beyond. Craig's throat was raw from screaming so much. His voice began to give out.

'Finally,' the man said. 'We're through.'

Craig looked down and saw the man pull a length of dirty material from his overalls. He quickly began wrapping it round what was left of Craig's thigh as a makeshift tourniquet.

'Just so you don't bleed out too quickly,' he said.

Then, after undoing the ankle bonds, the crazed man held his prize up high. Craig could see his own detached leg in the man's hands, one end no more than a jagged, bloody stump.

'Who wants first bite?'

'I do,' Henry said excitedly, raising his hand.

'You've already had a bite,' the man said. 'I got an idea.'

He set the leg and cleaver down on the table and picked up what looked like a strong carving knife. He then cut a thick slice from the top of the thigh, like carving turkey meat, and held it out to Tim.

'I know you ain't getting much, boy,' the man said to his son, 'but for all you do for this family, this is the least you should get in return. First taste. And one day, you'll get your fill, I promise you that. You'll get your fill and everything that comes with it.'

Tim actually looked touched, and he gratefully took the

meat. He brought it to his mouth and bit down, sloppily chewing into it.

It was too much for Craig.

The pain.

The sight of these people cutting into him.

Seeing a person, who could have been a friend, start to eat him alive.

The feeling of violation was staggering.

Craig wanted to pass out. Surely he had gone through enough? Surely the pain alone should have been sufficient to knock him out?

But no such luck. Whatever horrible fate God had planned for him, the twisted son of a bitch obviously wanted Craig to experience every last second.

The sucking and slurping noises from Tim, as he greedily devoured his food, made Craig want to vomit. Hell, everything he'd experienced this night made him want to throw up. But he didn't. He just continued to writhe and moan, helplessly.

It was all he could do.

The bearded man then started cutting off more from Craig's detached leg and served up a section to his wife.

'Thank you, dear,' she said to him. She then looked over to Craig and flashed him a crooked smile and a wink. 'And thank you, honey. I'm willing to bet this is going to be very tasty.'

She bit down, still maintaining eye contact with him, and yanked a chunk free. She chewed, slowly and deliberately, savouring the taste. Her eyes closed and she let out an appreciative moan.

'Oh boy,' she said, spitting small chunks as she spoke. 'I was right. This is delicious.'

'Come on,' Henry said, bouncing up and down on his heels, 'I've been waiting long enough. When is it my turn?'

'Soon,' the older man said impatiently. 'But you go last, because you can't control yourself.'

The man then carefully cut off another piece, slightly bigger than the previous two. 'I'm gonna need more than that,' Henry said.

'I know you are,' the man said. 'You always do. It's how you ended up so damn big.'

'Ain't my fault,' the brute said. 'Can't help the hunger inside of me.'

'True enough,' the man said, nodding. 'But you should learn to control it. Anyway, this piece ain't for you.'

The man held the newly cut slice in one hand and studied it. He then looked over to Henry, who was watching him like a greedy dog, salivating, waiting for his turn. The man shook his head and lifted the detached leg in his free hand. Craig saw exposed red flesh where the man had cut strips free.

'Here,' he said and threw the entire leg over to his bulbous son.

Henry was large, and powerful, but obviously not very nimble. In his excitement, he spilled and dropped the appendage and it rolled across the dirt floor, gathering up bits of dust and grime. The giant quickly grabbed it and held it out before him, an excited grin on his face, like a kid with a present on Christmas morning.

'Thanks, Da,' he said and bit down, mashing his stubby teeth through the skin. Blood ran free and slopped down his face. He pulled his head back, bringing a mouthful of meat away with it, and chewed greedily. He closed his eyes and let out a long, satisfied moan. He swallowed and took bite after bite, like he was quickly working his way through a chicken leg.

That was enough for Craig. He instinctively turned his head and threw up across the table.

'Awww, don't worry about that,' the woman said, trying to sound sincere, but unable to repress a slight giggle. 'It always happens. Nothing to be embarrassed about, dear boy.'

After coughing up some additional bile, Craig desperately tried to beg some more.

'Please,' he croaked, 'just end it. I can't take it any more.'

The woman approached him, still eating. 'Can't do that, sweetie,' she said. 'We need you alive. That's when you taste the best.' She then brought a bloodied hand down and traced her fingers along his remaining thigh, letting them dance up his skin.

The touch made Craig flinch, which in turn made her giggle again.

She ran her hands farther up, eyeing his body as she did. Then her hand hovered over his groin and Craig felt his body impulsively tighten up. She flicked her eyes up, meeting his own, and winked. 'Suppose there are ways to make this more bearable for you'

'Adela,' the bearded man spat. 'Stop that. Now.'

'You shut the fuck up!' she yelled back, not even looking at him. She continued to lock eyes with Craig. He gave a sudden intake of breath as her finger brushed against his member. 'Would you like that, sweetie?' she asked, trying to make her voice as seductive as possible.

Craig felt dizzy.

What the hell was wrong with her? In what realm of crazy did she have to live in to think he would want anything like that done to him while he was being eaten alive? Let alone from someone like her. She stroked it again, still smiling, her lips red and wet with blood.

Craig just shook his head, hoping his mind would break. Maybe then he could be free of this nightmare and get lost in sweet insanity.

The woman didn't take too kindly to his rebuttal. 'Why?' she asked. 'Something wrong with me? Too much woman for you?'

'Just leave me alone,' Craig said softly. 'Please. Just stop all this. I'm begging you.'

The woman curled her top lip into a scowl. 'Are you fucking stupid, boy? Take a look around you. Does it look like we have any intention of stopping? Have you seen how Henry is chomping down on that leg of yours? It's going to happen, we're going to eat you all up, and it's going to hurt. Now,' she went on, as her face softened and her stroking continued, 'what I'm offering is a way to take your mind off things.'

Craig began to weep. The whole situation was beyond fucked up. Did she really think her advances would do any good whatsoever? Kim could be stroking him right now, but with the pain he was in there was no chance of any kind of sexual reaction.

The woman seemed to notice his lack of arousal too. 'Hmmm, it's not playing. Why isn't it playing?'

'Please,' Craig repeated, shutting his eyes. 'Please, just stop. I can't take it any more. Just end it if you're going to.'

He knew it was hopeless, but he had nothing else to offer.

'Fucking prick,' the woman said, exploding into anger. She bent forward and her hand quickly found his balls and squeezed tight, causing him to squeal in fresh agony. His eyes shot open so wide he thought they would pop from his skull. 'Does this thing even work? I bet it doesn't.' She squeezed again. 'So, if it don't work, might as well get rid of it,' she said, turning to the bearded man. 'Ted? Pass me a knife. A big one. One that will get things a little messy.'

The man chuckled and picked up a knife, one with a serrated edge, and held it out for his wife, directly over Craig's body.

'No,' he pleaded. 'Don't. Please don't. I'm begging you. Please, for the love of God, just let it end.' He was screaming now, totally manic, and yet the man and woman, the two evil bastards who held his fate in their hands, just laughed. The woman took the serrated knife and looked it over.

'Ohhhh,' she said, 'good choice.'

She then leaned in again to Craig, bringing her head close to his, so he could make out every feature on her face; the sores, the wrinkles on her dirty skin, the milky, pale eyes, and the yellowed teeth. It all repulsed him.

'Now,' she said. 'I'm sorry to say this, honey, but I expect this will hurt quite a bit. But we can't let anything go to waste, anything at all, even down to the last small mouthful. Which is about all your little friend down there would measure up to.'

Craig began to scream for help. Another useless gesture, but he was beyond desperate.

'Keep screaming,' the older man said. 'Won't help you any, but damn if we don't enjoy the sound. Makes all of this a little bit more fun, you know.'

Craig barely heard him, he just continued to scream and thrash around uselessly on the table.

To make matters worse, the woman held up the knife directly in front of him, letting him take in every detail. He continued to scream.

'Time to get to carving, don't you think?' she asked him,

then stepped back a little. She centred beside him, near his crotch. 'Should have taken me up on my offer, boy. I'm good, you know. You would have enjoyed it.'

She grabbed a handful, pulled it up as far as she could, and swung the knife towards it.

Craig screamed again.

The agony was immeasurable.

And still he did not pass out.

28

ASHLEY WASN'T sure if she was in some kind of hell.

Images and scenes played out; horrible scenarios that she just couldn't get away from. Waking up with Tim, lying in a large, warm bed. She felt so happy that they were together and in love.

Then he struck her.

And tied her down as she struggled in vain.

His face changed, twisting somehow. His top lip pulled itself up to meet his nose and his eyes began to sag. There was a knock at the bedroom door, a room she didn't recognise.

At least it's clean, she thought.

Only a moment later, it wasn't. It changed into a filthy wreck of a room, with junk piled everywhere and the skeletal bodies of animals strewn across the floor.

They were large animals, and the skulls looked decidedly human.

Tim walked to the door and pulled it open with a slow squeak.

'Hey, babe,' he said, 'you're here.' He then stood aside as Kim entered, a big smile on her face.

'Oh, you have her tied up already,' she said. 'Kinky. Do we get to play now?'

'We sure do,' he said, and they kissed.

Then there was another knock at the door, but no one needed to answer it this time, it opened on its own. More people entered; a man with a scruffy beard and a cleft lip, a woman Ashley knew to be his wife, and a large, hulking thing.

'Everyone's here,' Kim said, pleased.

'So, let's make a start,' said the mountainous fat man with the cherubic face.

They all gathered round Ashley as she screamed.

Then things changed again.

She felt herself dragged upwards, as if being brought to the surface of an expanse of water.

It took her a moment to realise that reality was once again flooding her senses.

She felt movement, a sway from side to side, and she was aware of cold air against her skin. There was a throbbing pain in the back of her head which overpowered the other aches and strains in her body that also screamed for attention.

She slowly opened her eyes.

It was disorientating at first as things slowly came into a nauseating focus.

The man, who had seemed ready to end her life before she blacked out, was now carrying her, and she was once again completely tied up.

Which meant he had decided against killing her.

For now.

Ashley lifted her head a little, though the small movement caused more nausea and pain. There was no one behind them, but she could hear someone walking ahead, sniffling every now and again.

Kim.

There didn't seem to be anyone else with them, or if there was, they were moving silently. Which meant the woman Ashley had gutted had been left behind. Perhaps Ashley's attack had been enough to kill her?

Regardless of whatever grow-a-new-ass properties these freaks seemed to have, surely slicing open her stomach and cutting into the brain like that would be enough to make things permanent? Then again, the faceless man seemed to still be operating with a hole in his head and his brains scrambled. How they managed to survive such things was beyond Ashley, and she was pretty sure it always would be.

The pounding in the back of her head seemed to be growing worse, and she let out a woozy moan.

'Ah,' the man said, without stopping or altering his movements, 'looks like someone's awake. Have to say, girlie, you impressed me a little back there. Did a real good job on my sister. Going to be a while before she is back to normal and able to get herself home.'

Back to normal? After that? How was that even fucking possible?

People weren't built to get back to normal after suffering such wounds. Certainly not without immediate medical attention and a shit ton of luck.

'What are you people?' Ashley asked.

'Just a family,' the man answered, 'doing what we need to do to get by.'

'No,' Ashley said, still woozy. 'I mean, how come nothing can hurt you?'

'Things hurt us plenty, I guarantee you that. You think

Claudia isn't in pain after what you did to her? Shit, she'll be feeling that for months.'

'But she isn't dead.'

'No,' he said, 'she isn't. Takes a little more than that to put us down for good.'

'How is that possible?'

The man laughed. 'People don't tend to find that out, it's kind of a trade secret.' Ashley stayed silent, knowing she'd wasted her time asking. To her surprise, the man actually carried on. 'But you may well get to know. Have some things to talk to Mother and Father about when I get back. About you, actually. Might be that you end up finding out more about us than most do.'

Ashley had no idea what that meant and had no desire to find out, though she knew she wouldn't get a lot of say in the matter.

'Are you human?' she asked.

The man seemed to pause. 'Yes,' he said finally. 'We're human, just come to be a little... different, is all. Everyone is different, though, aren't they? Different is what makes the world go round.'

'It does,' Ashley said, 'but not when it turns you into a killer. Or a cannibal.'

'Well, that's your opinion,' he said. 'For now at least. I have a feeling you might come to change your mind. I should have killed you back there, you know, after what you did to my sister. But I didn't. Decided to take a chance on you.'

'That's awful big of you. Am I supposed to thank you?'

'Not yet, but in time you just might.'

'I wouldn't count on it.'

'We'll see,' he said. 'But I think you might be surprised, given what we can offer.'

Ashley wanted to tell him to go fuck himself, but thought better of it. It was pointless antagonising him any further.

She heard Kim sniffle again, up ahead, and wondered what she made of the conversation she had no doubt overheard. From the sounds of things, Kim was walking on ahead of her own accord. And if that was the case, she had much more freedom and movement than Ashley did. If any of them had a chance to try something, it was her.

'Kim?' Ashley called. 'Are you okay?'

'No talking,' the man snapped.

Ashley ignored him. 'Kim, talk to me.'

'I said shut up,' the man snapped. 'I'm warning you both, don't try anything.'

'Ashley,' Kim answered in a quivering voice. 'Just do what he says. He'll kill us.'

'That's a good girl,' Ted said and slapped Ashley on the back of her leg. 'See, you should listen to your friend.'

'He's going to kill us anyway, Kim,' Ashley said. 'You need to run, if you can. Try to get away.'

Ashley suddenly felt herself flip forward and land hard on her back, the force of the drop knocking the wind from her.

'What did I just say?' the man yelled, grabbing the handle of his machete and pulling it free. He held the tip of it to Ashley's face. 'Do you need me to prove my point? I've already been lenient with you, but I swear, another word from you,' he then raised the blade and pointed it to Kim, 'and I gut your friend. Nice and slow.'

Ashley looked up and saw Kim ahead, her hands tied behind her back and a makeshift leash running back to the man. Pure fear was etched on the girl's face.

'Ashley,' she pleaded, 'just do as he says.'

Ashley knew that doing as he said meant being lead to their deaths, only being quiet about it. If that was the case, what was the worst that could happen if they at least tried something? Worst case, they met their end a little earlier than they could have, but this freak and his family wouldn't get the pleasure of eating them alive, which seemed to be his plan.

At least it would be on their terms.

If there was anything left for Ashley to cling to in this life, that was as good as it was going to get.

But her friend was pleading with her, begging her to just... what? Give up?

Where was the fight she'd insisted Ashley show?

Maybe Kim was playing for as much time as she could, delaying death, hoping for some divine intervention, but as Kim herself had said earlier, that wasn't going to happen.

No one would save them, so they had to save themselves.

But there was nothing Ashley could do. She was bound up tight and totally at this man's mercy. He seemed stronger than his sister, and she got the feeling he would have no trouble carrying her the rest of the way back to the house.

If Kim had truly given up, then there was nothing to be done, other than to let this man lead them back to his house.

To their deaths.

To become nothing more than a meal to these deranged lunatics.

'Are you going to stay quiet?' the man asked. Ashley stared daggers at him, but slowly nodded. 'Good,' he said and again lifted her to his shoulder. 'We ain't far away now, anyway.'

Soon they were moving again.

On their way to their slaughter.

To say Ashley was disappointed to see her friend totally broken, after all Kim's talk of fighting on to the bitter end, was an understatement.

Only a little while ago, the situation had been reversed, but Ashley had, after some persuasion, stepped up, whereas Kim had now regressed.

'There we are,' the man said, stopping. Ashley pulled her head up and looked over his shoulder. Through the darkness, she could just make out the house up in the distance.

The man took a breath.

'Home sweet home.'

29

After the woman had finished hacking away Craig's manhood—and pulled it free to dangle it mockingly before him—things descended into a hellish chaos.

Whereas before the family had waited for the father to serve up their portions, the woman's actions had changed things; tipping them over the edge and completely unleashing all of their animalistic desires.

Formalities were dispensed with.

'Okay,' the father said, 'everyone dig in and help themselves.'

And they did.

Craig lay sobbing, in unspeakable agony, as everyone moved in. Everyone accept Tim. He just stood by, with a long face, and watched as the rest of them got to work.

The feeling of the three of them starting to devour him at the same time, pulling and tearing and cutting and biting, was pain on a completely new scale. The agony was everywhere, in different shades and measures.

He screamed; a continuous, terrible, desperate bellowing that did not stop.

He felt the cleaver go to work again on the opposite side of his body, this time on an arm. It again sunk into the flesh, just above his bicep, again and again, until his arm came free. There was no carving of the meat this time, the father simply dug in, like Henry had done with his leg before.

Craig also felt a tearing sensation in his gut. Looking down, he saw the great, fat beast that was Henry dig his fingers through the skin of Craig's stomach. They punctured through, with piercing pain, and pulled, tearing Craig open.

The big, meaty hands then submerged inside of him, and Craig saw glistening, snakelike, red and purple intestines pulled free. Henry lifted them to his face and forced them into his mouth, slurping them up.

The mother, who had just stripped him of his manhood, reached in as well, stealing more of his insides.

The horror was just too much for him, and something fractured. It was as if his mind split into two.

Part of it was present in the moment, feeling the pain his dying body was put through. The other was aware of what was going on, but was more detached and took everything in, noticing certain, surreal details.

Henry made his way to Craig's head, still slurping in strings of meat. He reached a fat, bloodstained hand down to Craig's face.

To his eye.

Craig felt the fumbling, cumbersome appendages work against his eyeball, attempting to pluck it free, but instead only succeeding in pushing it farther in.

Craig's incomprehensible screeches grew louder.

'I can never get these things out,' Henry said, his mouth full.

'Cos your fingers are too big,' the father said and pointed

to the side table where the instruments of death were still laid out. 'Use that thin needle thing.'

Thin needle thing?

The detached half of Craig's mind noticed the term, which wasn't the most technical. It was almost comical. However, it was clear Henry understood and grabbed an instrument that was exactly like his father had described.

Craig could only watch as the sharp end of the long needle came down towards him. He shut his eyes, but knew that would give no respite. He felt the needle sink into the corner of his socket.

He thrashed and yelled, but evidently this was music to the family's ears. They laughed as they ate. The woman even danced around, wrapping some of his innards around her shoulders like a shawl.

The needle went in farther, then angled itself, and pulled back again in an effort to pop the eyeball free.

The pain was excruciating, but the needle slipped free without success.

'Damn it,' Henry said.

'Try again,' his mother told him. 'You'll get it. Second time lucky.'

He did try again and, as his mother had promised, the second time was lucky.

Craig felt the eyeball dislodge and slip from his skull. He opened his remaining eye, but his vision was split. There was a further pull, accompanied by a stinging sensation inside of his head. Something snapped and his vision again became whole.

No, not whole.

Halved.

Henry had pulled the eyeball free.

Craig could see the red tendrils of the optic nerve dangling down above him.

Henry studied it, then held it up for his mother to see. 'I see you,' he said, laughing.

His mother broke into hysterics. 'Oh, Henry, you're so funny.'

Henry nodded, clearly in agreement. He then popped the eyeball into his mouth, like a piece of candy, and began to chew. Craig heard a squelch as the monster's powerful jaws clamped shut.

'Juicy,' he said and let out a moan of satisfaction.

And so the horror carried on.

Craig's screams eventually died off after the mother had done something with his Adams apple. Craig couldn't see exactly what, but he knew his throat was a mess. His jaw still worked though, moving up and down, trying to let loose a noise, a release, that would just not come.

His vision began to blur, and a lightheadedness started to take over. After being so alert through all of the torture, an alertness probably caused by the searing pain, it was a relief to know that it was clearly coming to an end for him.

His horrific injuries were finally bringing death.

Craig felt the needle plunge into the corner of his other eye, ready to rob him of his sight completely.

Come on, he prayed to any God that was listening. *End it now. It's time. End it now.*

A small part of him was actually thankful they seemed to be devouring him so completely. If there was nothing left of him, it meant his family would never know what had happened.

At least they would be spared that horror.

Unless, of course, Kim and Ashley had gotten away.

And he dearly hoped they had. He couldn't stand the

thought of them, especially Kim, going through this agony and torture.

It was a small mercy that she wasn't here to see him like this.

Then, as if God was quite happy to shit on him further, he heard it.

'Craig!'

Craig felt the pressure on the needle release, and he was able to turn his head. Through blurred, unclear vision, he managed to make out the shape of the person who was screaming.

No. Please God, no.

It was Kim.

One final *fuck you* from whatever twisted karma was orchestrating this whole weekend.

He tried to call back to her, but could make no sound.

Finally, death claimed him.

THE SIGHT of inhuman carnage inflicted on her boyfriend when Kim entered the room was enough to make her drop to her knees.

It was monstrous; absolute desecration. The metallic smell of blood filled the room, bathing her in its stink.

The other members of the family stood around a great stone table. All of them smeared in blood and gore, chewing noisily.

Feasting on him.

As if what they were doing was the most normal thing in the world.

As they ate, Craig's body twitched and moved very slowly, as if it were about to give out.

Blood flowed steadily from every part of his ruined torso, bubbling free in multiple streams. A bloody stump indicated one of his arms was completely gone, and she could see another stump beyond, where a leg should be. His stomach was pulled open all the way up to his chest, revealing what was left of his insides, and also part of his rib cage.

The hideous sight was too much for Kim, and she couldn't help but call out Craig's name. Henry was doing something to his face, but upon hearing her yell, he smiled and stepped back.

Craig turned his face towards her.

One eye was completely gone, leaving an empty pit in its place, and the other was bulging from its socket unnaturally, almost like a sickening cartoon. He tried to say something, but his jaw simply moved, like a fish devoid of water. Then he slumped back, unmoving, dying before her eyes.

Kim began to scream and scream and scream, pulling at her hair in absolute terror.

Through it all, she managed to hear the words from the man who held her on a leash.

'You fuckers, you started without me.'

HE COULDN'T BELIEVE IT. The greedy pieces of shit couldn't have waited just a little while longer, just held out a little bit so that they could all eat together, like a family should.

'You and your sister were taking too long,' Father told him. 'Besides, we got two more to go at.'

He pointed to the two women Ted had in his charge.

'Not the point,' Ted said. 'You should have waited.'

'It's done now,' his father said.

'Ted?' Mother asked. 'Where is your sister?'

Ted chuckled. 'Funny story. This one here,' he let Ashley flop to the floor from his shoulder, 'has something about her. She managed to get free of Sis. Ended up driving Claudia's own knife into her skull. If it weren't for me, this one would have gotten away.'

'And what about your sister?' Mother asked.

'She's still out there, but she isn't in a good way.'

'You left her?'

'I couldn't bring them all back on my own, Mother,' he said defensively. 'If it weren't for Claudia, we would have been back by now. Her fuck up nearly cost us these two little rabbits. Anyway, she'll pull herself round. Eventually.'

'But she'll miss all this,' Mother said, opening her hands to the man who lay dead on the table.

'And that's her fault,' Ted said.

'He's got a point, Adela,' Father said, cutting in.

'But it's been so long. If she doesn't get to eat this time, how will she cope? Who knows how long it will be before we get to do this again.'

'Then she shouldn't have fucked up,' Father said. 'We all have our jobs to do. And we all need to do them well for this to work. Sounds like she got sloppy, so she needs to understand the consequences of that.'

'But she'll be a nightmare to deal with,' Mother said.

'Then we'll lock her in the basement. I'm sure Henry can help straighten her out.'

Henry smiled and nodded, still too preoccupied with eating to talk. He had plucked the boy's remaining eyeball free and shoved it into his maw.

'Well,' Ted said, 'I might have half an idea about that.'

'What do you mean, son?' his father asked, genuinely curious.

Ted kicked out at the redhead who, he noted, had rolled over and was looking at what was left of her friend. Her face was unreadable. She wasn't howling and screaming like her frantic companion.

'This one,' he sneered. 'She has something about her, like I said. Not like most we get who are only good for food.'

'Are you saying what I think you are?' Father asked. Ted shrugged.

'Not sure,' he replied. 'But figured it was worth, you know, seeing what you thought. And...' he trailed off.

'And what?'

'And, if you thought the same, maybe we could go see what Grandpa thinks too.'

His father fell silent and began to run a hand through his beard, now coated red with blood and flesh.

'That's a lot of mouths to feed,' Mother said. 'Can we handle another?'

'I don't think we can,' Father said. 'It's hard enough as it is now.'

'So then,' Mother asked, 'what is there to discuss? More food for tonight. That's all there is to it.'

But Ted could see his father mulling it over and had a feeling the old man was coming to the same conclusion he had earlier.

'Ted might have a point here,' Father said.

'What kind of point?'

'Well, it's been a while since we've changed things up,' he replied. 'Timothy has been the runt for too long. It's about time he got the chance to get what he's owed. Only way to do that is to bring someone new into the family. Take in a new child to cover his role and let him move up. And this one looks pretty enough to be good bait. Hell, even with that gash across her face I bet she could bring us lots of fresh food. This might be a good opportunity, if Ted is right about her, that is.'

'But we've just said we can't take on another mouth. Are you implying what I think you are?'

'Maybe.'

'Are you serious? Are you really saying that we just cut one of the children loose? How can you say that? They won't be able to cope or survive on their own.'

'We don't cut them loose, we take em' down to see their Grandpa.'

'That's even worse,' Mother said. 'You're talking about killing them. And who would you suggest?'

'Well, Claudia got sloppy, and it's her fault that one of them nearly got away. Everyone knows there are consequences for failure. It might be good to make an example. Show that the rules aren't to be broken.'

'But she's our daughter,' Mother said, 'how can you be so careless?'

'Not saying it's an easy decision, but the right ones rarely are. We gotta do what's right for the family as a whole. We're stagnating here, Adela, you can see that. And the man downstairs won't allow that forever. This could be what we need.'

Adela approached the redhead, who had pushed herself up to her knees. The girl stared back at the older woman with a look of disgust and defiance. Adela grabbed the younger girl by the chin and tilted her head up to inspect her face.

'Fuck you,' the redhead said, drawing a chuckle from Ted.

'Looks to have fight in her. Thought she was the quiet one?' Adela asked, looking over to Timothy.

He shrugged. 'I thought so too.'

'You can all go to hell,' the girl said. 'Do you really think I would want to be part of your fucked up family? After the things I've seen you do?'

'Oh,' Adela said, 'that won't be a problem. If we think you're Webb material, then you'll join us after you see the old man. No question about it. It's not exactly a choice, dear. Do you think we've always been like this? Fuck no. I was a good, church-going young lady once. But if Grandpa sees a certain something in you, a certain... quality, then he can grant you things and show you things you never dreamed possible. Things you had no idea existed. That's just how it works. Choice don't come into it. He just turns you. If you're lucky.'

'Bullshit,' the girl said.

Adela laughed and let go of her. 'You'll see in time, my dear.'

'So,' Father said, 'you agree?'

Adela cocked her head and Ted could see the contemplation on her face. 'Maybe. She might just have it. Though only the old man can know for sure.'

'So we take her to see him,' Father said with finality.

'And if he agrees, and she becomes one of us? What do we do with Claudia?'

'We wait till she gets herself back here,' Father said. 'Then take her down to see Grandpa as well.'

'What'll happen to her?' Timothy asked.

'Doesn't matter,' Father said. 'If he agrees with this, then after we take Claudia down we won't see her again. No need to worry ourselves about what he does with her.'

'What if he doesn't agree?' Henry asked, still picking bits from the body left on the table. He pulled chunks of meat free from the open stomach and slipped them into his mouth. 'What if she isn't one of us?'

'Then nothing happens,' Father said. 'We carry on as we are.'

'With Claudia around?' Henry asked.

'Of course,' Father replied.

'Don't think she will be too happy, though, when she finds out what we were thinking.'

Father shrugged. 'She'll learn to deal with it. She'll have to. And she should let it be a lesson not to fuck up. But, I have to say, I have a good feeling about this one,' he pointed to the redhead. 'Might be just what we are looking for.'

'So, what do we do first?' Ted asked. 'Do we finish up with her?' He pulled at the leash, making the Asian one yelp, a small break in her sobbing. 'Or do we take the redhead down to see Grandpa first?'

Father though about that for a moment before finally deciding.

'We take her to Grandpa,' he said. 'Timothy and Henry can stay up here and clean up. They'll need to get rid of the leftovers and set the table again, anyway. The rest of us will go down and see what's what.'

'Sounds good to me,' Ted said, then he leaned closer to the redhead, close enough to smell her. 'Good luck. If all goes well, looks like I'll be calling you sister soon enough.'

30

ASHLEY KNEW these people were insane, that much was painfully evident, but seeing what had become of poor Craig, a sight which turned her stomach, was enough to prove the family was completely and utterly unhinged.

Craig's body had been totally ravaged and mangled.

It was an inhuman sight.

The blood that ran from the ruined corpse drained from the table, which Ashley saw had small holes along its surface. His lifeblood slipping away to God knows where.

It was sickening.

In some respect, considering their mental state, the Webb's talk of getting her to join them, to become part of their nightmare, shouldn't seem that crazy. But did they really think she would ever allow that to happen? Even if it proved to be the only way to save her life, living like them was not an acceptable compromise.

She would rather die.

The man who had carried her back here, Ted, began cutting at her bonds.

'You're going to need a bit more movement,' he said. 'Getting down there isn't exactly easy.'

She'd expected him to perhaps free up her legs, but to untie her completely surprised her. She looked at him warily.

'You'd be advised not to try anything stupid here, girl,' the father said and folded his arms over his chest. The tone he gave off was scalding, almost... parental.

She felt Ted grab her from behind. He wrapped one arm tightly around her chest and brought up his knife to her throat.

'I'd listen to him carefully if I were you, sweetheart,' she heard him say, feeling his rotten breath on the side of her face.

He pushed her forward and the older man, Benjamin, pulled a key from his overall pocket and walked to the corner of the room, where he squatted down. As Ashley passed the table where Craig's remains sat, she saw Benjamin fumbling with something on the floor; a thick, iron grate, roughly about three foot by three foot. He unlocked it and placed the key back into the pocket on his chest, then opened the grate, which was hinged at one side.

A trap door.

So that's how they proposed to get her down there. Ted then pushed Ashley over to his father, who grabbed her by the throat.

'Ready to go see the old man?' he asked with a sneer.

'Wait,' a voice shouted, echoing around the small space. Everyone turned their attentions back to Kim, who had been forgotten. She was in a sitting position on the floor, pulling her tied hands under her butt, before bending her legs and looping her arms from under them. She didn't seem to be in any kind of rush.

'You got something to say?' the father asked, chuckling.

'Take me instead,' she said, standing to her feet.

'Take you? Take you where?'

'Down there,' she said. 'Wherever you are going. Take me. Let me join you.'

Benjamin threw his head back and let out a bellowing laugh.

'You? Join us? Oh, my dear, I'm afraid that isn't how this works,' he said.

'And you wouldn't fit in, anyway,' Adela added. 'You're eyes are too slanty. Not really *our sort*.'

She laughed as she spoke, and Henry chuckled along with her.

'Besides,' Benjamin went on, 'you don't just get to ask. You need to be chosen.'

'Then choose me,' she said, taking a step forward.

'Why should we do that?'

'Because,' she said, still walking forward. No one seemed concerned by her, merely curious. 'I have what it takes. I can be one of you.'

Ted quickly walked over to Kim and took a strong hold of her.

'Wait,' Benjamin commanded, seemingly intrigued. Ted released her and stepped aside. 'So,' Ben went on, 'you think you have what it takes to be one of us? Well, I have to say, in all my years, never have I heard anyone say they actually *want* to join us. Like I said, it's never a choice.'

'But I want to,' Kim said.

Ashley couldn't believe what she was hearing from her so-called friend. Surely what they'd done to Craig sickened Kim's as much as it did her? Surely she could have nothing but contempt for these people? Then, Ashley thought back to Kim's earlier eagerness to leave her behind, and figured this was just another display of desperate selfishness. She was doing it for one reason and one reason only: so she didn't have to die.

'No, you don't want to. You just don't want to die,' the man said, as if reading Ashley's thoughts. 'And it isn't going to work, I'm afraid.'

'That's not it,' Kim insisted. 'I do want to be one of you. And I can prove it.'

'Prove it? How?'

Kim continued walking, slowly, up to the table, up to the bloodied and destroyed body of Craig. Everyone, including Ashley, watched her intently. After taking a deep breath, Kim then lowered her head forward to Craig's opened stomach and opened her mouth.

Jesus, no, Ashley thought to herself, repulsed. Surely there was no way Kim would go through with it.

But she did.

Ashley almost gagged as she watched Kim bury her face into Craig's insides. She heard a wet squelch, and Kim brought her head back up. Her mouth was smeared with blood, and glistening strings dangled from it. She then began to chew, slowly.

'How could you?' Ashley said.

Kim didn't answer, just continued chewing. The family erupted in laughter.

'Jesus, Timothy,' Benjamin said, doubling over in laughter. 'You really did bring us quite the selection this time. I've never seen anything like it.'

'I don't know what to say,' Tim said. 'I never knew either of them had it in them. Maybe I misjudged them.'

Kim smiled as she chewed. It was a manic sight, and she made her way over to Craig's head. 'What's the best part to eat?' she asked through a mouthful of meat. 'The throat looks tasty.'

Ashley had half an idea to race over to Kim and strangle her herself.

Kim leaned in to Craig again, ready to take another bite as the family continued to roar in laughter around her.

Ashley was horrified. After all she'd seen, this sickened her the most, purely because of the betrayal of it all. Her mind was racing with confusion and rage, and it took her a moment to realise Kim was staring directly at her.

Kim's eyes flicked from Ashley, then to the trap door, then back again, and she gave an almost imperceptible nod.

Ashley realised Kim was signalling to her.

She wanted her to go down there.

But when, and why?

And then it all became clear.

Kim, with her hands still tied together, quickly grabbed what looked like a sharp kitchen knife from the small table next to the slab. She screamed with fury and sprinted towards Benjamin, the knife held out before her. The family, still recovering from their laughing fit, were slow to react, and Kim lunged, thrusting the knife into the man's throat. Ashley heard a wet squelch as the metal slid easily into the flesh. The blade was of such a length that it penetrated right through and came out of the back of Benjamin's neck.

Kim quickly sidestepped around him, still holding the knife and twisting the man as she moved, putting Ashley behind her, and her between Ashley and the rest of the family. She pulled the knife free and lunged into Benjamin. They tangled briefly until Kim pushed him backwards into Tim, who caught the older man before he fell. Benjamin brought a hand up to his neck, his eyes wide with shock, and pressed it tight to the puncture wound, trying and stem the blood that gushed and spurted free. It was useless, though, as it pumped rhythmically from between his fingers. Benjamin sank to his knees.

Excitement spread through the rest of the family, the violence like an aphrodisiac to them. Henry whooped and hollered, clapping his hands together.

'Very clever,' the mother said, pulling her lips back into something halfway between a smile and a grimace. 'Not going to do much good, though.'

Kim turned her head slightly, looking back to Ashley.

'Go,' she whispered.

'But—' Ashley began, but didn't have the chance to finish. Kim backed up and shoved Ashley, who stumbled. She lost her footing on the edge of the trap door and fell inside. The drop was only a few feet, but she landed painfully on the earthy floor.

She heard commotion above and saw Kim drop the knife down to her before slamming the grate shut. A metallic clang rang out as Ashley tried to catch up with what was happening. Kim pressed herself into the grate and was frantically working her hands as bodies descended on top of her. It took Ashley a moment to understand what she was doing; in her hands, she had the same key Benjamin had used when he opened the grate, and she was now locking it.

Ashley realised she must have taken it when she was wrestling with Benjamin, before shoving him away.

Seemingly all part of a desperate plan.

Frantic yelling rose in volume and intensity from above, a yelling that was overpowered by Kim's screaming. She was in pain, then Ashley saw why. A blade appeared though her front, just to the side of her stomach. Still her hands worked and Ashley heard a metallic click.

The grate had been successfully locked.

Thick, fat hands wrapped around Kim's throat, hands that engulfed her neck almost completely, and began to squeeze. Kim's eyes bulged and her screams were choked off, but that did not slow her down. She thrust an arm through the grate and something fell from her grip, landing close to Ashley.

It was the key.

Ashley looked up at her friend who mouthed the words *I'm sorry*, before being dragged completely from view.

Screams of pain and agony rang out, along with the frantic, arguing voices of the family. Tim appeared at the grate above her and pressed himself down on to it. He looked furious.

'Don't you fucking go anywhere,' he said. 'We will gut you, you hear? We will fucking tear you apart.'

Ashley picked up both the key and the knife that Kim had dropped. Kim's last act had been to save her friend's life and give her a chance at escape.

Ashley felt a draft to her side and saw she was at the start of some kind of small tunnel, only a few feet in circumference, that cut down into the earth at a steady decline. She didn't know where it led, and she guessed something would be waiting, but at least it got her away from the horrors above, from this psychopathic family, and maybe gave her a chance at freedom.

And it was all thanks to Kim, a girl she had thought to be a coward and a traitor.

A girl who had sacrificed her own life for Ashley.

Ashley looked back up to the face of the man she once thought she loved.

'Tim,' she shouted up, then raised a hand, middle finger extended. 'Fuck you.'

She then began to crawl onwards as quickly as she could, down the decline of the tunnel, one that grew ever steeper.

Behind her, she could still hear the threats and cursing of Tim as she left him behind.

31

THE PAIN WAS IMMENSE, but Kim felt an odd sensation of peace through it all. With her throat crushed, she lay gasping on the floor. The knife that punctured through her had been pulled out, but it had ripped and split things on its way. She felt blood spit out of the gaping holes, front and back, with every breath her dying body took.

It was the kind of pain she had been fearing, the reason she had considered running and leaving her friend behind, all so she could save herself. After the carnage and violence back in the woods and seeing Ashley drive that knife into the woman's skull, but not killing her, something had broken inside her. If something like that didn't kill them, then nothing would. It seemed to snuff out all hope of escape, so a new survival instinct took over; compliance.

She stopped resisting and fell in line, submitting herself to these beasts in the hope that they would spare her. She didn't really believe they would, but what else could she do?

Then, after being lead back on a leash like a dog, she saw what they had done to Craig, and she knew that was to be her fate. Whilst Ashley had shown the kind of fight they needed, Kim had wilted when it had mattered.

The agony she was in, the pain she had been so scared of, was far worse than she had imagined it could be. However, despite that, it still didn't compare to the shame she felt at her previous actions.

So, when these people had talked about getting Ashley to join them, something that still didn't make sense to Kim, she had made a decision. She was going to fight hell-for-leather to ensure that at least one of them got out of here alive. Or, at least give one of them a chance.

And she had succeeded.

Right now, her friend had that chance. It may not have been much, and she could very well still meet a nasty end, but at least she'd given Ashley hope.

And maybe earned her forgiveness as well.

Kim felt Henry step over her, his towering bulk rising up and up. She could see his fat head looking down at her from up high with a scowl as she struggled to suck in pained breaths.

'What do we do with her?' he asked. 'She's dying. Cold meat is no good.'

The man she had stabbed, Benjamin, was on his feet again, trying to talk, but he could do no more than gargle and spit blood. The crimson liquid still spilled liberally from the vicious wound, and he looked incredibly pale.

Good, thought Kim, proud of her achievement.

'Forget her,' the woman said. 'Kill her and be done with it. We need to get after the other one, and quick.'

Henry smiled. 'Looks like your time's up,' he said. 'Shame we don't get a proper meal from you.'

'Henry,' his mother snapped, 'this is no time for playing around. Get on with it. We need you.'

'Okay, Ma,' he said defensively, like a temperamental teenager. He then reached down and took hold of Kim's neck. 'This is going to hurt,' he whispered.

And it did.

His mighty hands compressed, crushing Kim's already mashed throat utterly and completely. She felt a sudden pain as her head was twisted sharply to the side. Something cracked, but death wasn't instant. Kim was unable to open her mouth to scream and her head wobbled uselessly in his grip.

There was an almighty tug, and she actually felt the vertebrae in her neck pull apart as the skin surrounding it stretched and split.

Kim's last feeling was of rising into the air as her body lay motionless on the floor below.

'GET OUT OF THE WAY,' Ted said, pushing Timothy aside as his brother spat obscenities down into the dark void, but the girl was gone, that much was clear. Ted began working at the grate, digging the long blade of his machete around the edge of it, into the ground, hoping, in vain, he could dig it up. Without the key, he could think of no other way to gain access.

And the only key he was aware of for that grate was down there below them.

Ted was angry. Furious in fact, that his father, who had just given a speech on responsibility and consequences, had so stupidly lost the fucking key. Right now, she was heading farther down there, towards *him*, and they, with all their power, were actually powerless to stop her. It was the single biggest clusterfuck he had seen from anyone in his family. Ever.

If anyone deserved punishment for their actions, it was his father.

But Ted was also more than a little scared. Sure, his father had fucked up, but it was Ted who had first suggested turning the redhead, and that was the reason the grate had been opened in the first place.

So, would everything be blamed on him?

But just because Father had fucked up, royally fucked up, surely that didn't make him wrong about the girl. The fight she was showing had to be proof he was right? He hoped the family, and Grandpa, would see it that way too.

Regardless, the chances of the redhead joining them now were effectively finished. She was on her way down to where *he* lived and, where Grandpa was concerned, there were very specific rules. The chief of which was that no outsider went down there without a member of the family escorting them.

He was quite insistent on that. And he was going to be pissed.

Heads would roll, probably literally.

He prayed it wouldn't be his own.

No matter how much he tried to dig around the frame of the grate to create an opening that could perhaps pull the whole thing free, it was useless. The earth was just too thick, and the frame was set in too deep.

He needed another way.

He swivelled around, looking for something, anything, that would help. He saw Henry holding the Asian girl's head. Her jaw moved up and down a couple of times; an automated motor response, a hangover from life. Red tendrils fell from what remained of her neck and, through them, he saw a small length of spine.

The mouth stopped moving.

Henry studied the head, like it was a curiosity, and stared into the girl's eyes as her life drained away. He then tossed the head carelessly to his side. It bounced once and rolled from Ted's view.

'Ted,' his mother snapped, moving next to him. 'What are you waiting for? Keep digging. We need to get down there, now.'

But digging was pointless. Father stumbled about, trying to bark out orders, but was unable to speak. He only succeeded in covering the area with his still running blood. If things weren't so tense and urgent, it might have even been funny.

'Quiet down, you,' Mother said to him, a seething anger in her tone. 'This is all your fucking fault. How could you let one of them get the better of you like that? This has turned into one big fuck up.'

Father tried to say something, but it was useless. He couldn't speak and Mother wasn't listening. Ted was more than a little relieved Mother saw things his way, seemingly blaming only one person for all of this.

He looked back to the grate, then to Henry, and an idea formed.

'Keep going,' Mother said and slapped him painfully around the head.

'I'm not getting anywhere,' he shot back, 'but there might be another way.'

'What do you mean?'

'Henry,' he shouted over to his brother, who walked over to them. 'Need your help here, buddy. Up for a challenge?'

Henry laughed and clapped his hands. 'Always,' he said. 'What is it?'

'Need you to test your strength. There's no digging through this. So, do you think you'd be able to rip it open for us?'

Henry studied the grate, cocking his head to one side. 'Yeah,' he said. 'I think I can do that.'

Ted and his mother moved aside, giving Henry space to work. The giant reached down to the grate and took hold, setting himself and taking a deep breath.

He then heaved and let out a long, strained groan, pulling with everything he had. Small veins formed on his forehead and popped from his neck. He was pulling so hard his whole body was shaking.

'Careful you don't shit yourself,' Timothy said, smiling to himself.

'Shut up, boy,' Mother snapped, lashing out at him.

Henry was straining desperately, but Ted heard a small creak from the metal and saw the frame slowly begin to bend.

'Keep going, brother,' Ted said, giving encouragement. 'You're doing it. You're actually doing it. It's starting to give.'

Henry stopped and took a breath, his face beet red and sweating. He smiled and nodded at Ted, then set himself again. He drew in a few quick breaths and heaved once more. Ted again heard the sound of straining metal, louder this time. The thick iron frame bent and twisted in front of his eyes. Henry stopped again to get his breath.

'That's a good boy,' Mother said, rubbing Henry on the arm. 'Such a strong boy. You're doing me proud. One more, just one more and you might have it.'

Henry gritted his teeth together, his face a picture of determination. He gave an almighty roar and pulled again.

The lock broke.

Metal splintered with a squeal and the lid swung open, so fast the squatting Henry lost his balance and fell to his back, his legs sticking up in the air like a stuck turtle.

Mother cheered.

'Well done, Henry' she said, then pushed at Ted. 'Move. Get down there, after her.'

'You hear that, you fucking bitch,' Timothy yelled loudly into the hole. 'We're coming for you now. You're fucking dead.'

There was a lot of anger in Timothy, more so than usual, but Ted soon figured out why. Only moments ago, he'd been given hope that another member would come in to the family, one that would be ranked beneath him and take over his duties. And that would give him the chance to move up, and he would finally be able to feed fully.

With Father's fuck up, all of that hope had been yanked away.

Ted pushed him aside and dropped into the hole. His feet hit the floor and he dove forward onto his stomach and began to crawl forward into the tunnel as quickly as he could. He heard someone else drop in behind him.

The tunnel was small, but easy enough to navigate through. He did wonder if Henry would be able to squeeze his bulk through it, though. His much larger brother hadn't been down here since he had been turned all those years ago. Henry had been big then, but nothing like what he'd become.

Ted felt a vibration through the ground beneath him and heard a dull, heavy thud. He also heard his giant brother let out an *oomf* as he hit the floor. Clearly, Henry was going to try his luck.

Ted just hoped he didn't get stuck in the tunnel, as it was

the only way in or out. If he got wedged in good, then they'd have to cut their way through him to get back up.

Something, he supposed, that could be fun.

But first, they had work to do.

That redheaded bitch needed to die.

32

ASHLEY MADE her way through the tunnel on all fours as quickly as she could. The space was big enough for her, but it was pitch black and the air was starting to thin. The only thing she had to light the way was her phone, the thing that had been almost useless until now. She was using its torch feature, shining a light up ahead, but it had been days since its last charge and, even though it had been used sparsely, the battery was close to dead.

The tunnel itself seemed to be a natural one. It wasn't a perfect circle, not even close, so she doubted it had been purposefully dug. Clumps of dirt and rock surrounded her, and her palms and knees pressed painfully into stones and rocks as she moved. The decline was steadily increasing, and it had begun to put a strain on her wrists as she used them to stop her body weight from slipping forward. If the slope increased much more she wouldn't need to crawl, she would simply slide down the tunnel.

Her face still stung from where the younger woman had knifed her earlier. Other cuts and bruises also sung for attention. Ashley was hurt and physically exhausted.

She thought of Kim.

Whatever had happened over these last few hours, the only thing she could think of now was her friend's last, selfless act. And the words she had mouthed as those monstrous hands grabbed her.

I'm sorry.

Her sacrifice had given Ashley the opportunity to escape, so it didn't matter how tired she was, how much pain she was in, she had to keep going.

She owed it to her friend.

The sound of the family's bickering and Tim's furious taunts faded more as she put further distance between them. And she was happy to let it drown out.

But then she heard something that spurred her on faster. A loud, metal screech, and more shouting from Tim. She couldn't be sure what he said, but she knew that somehow they were through, and they were after her.

Ashley knew how quickly they could move, especially in these kinds of environments. It was almost inhuman. It meant they would gain on her, there was no question of that.

Her only hope was if she'd already put enough distance between them to get to the end of this tunnel before they caught up with her.

The knife Kim had dropped for her was wedged into the back of Ashley's trousers, and she could feel the blade cut against the skin of her buttocks as she crawled. Regardless, she didn't move it, and she didn't adjust. Instead, she used the constant stinging as motivation to move faster.

The key for the grate was also tucked into her pocket as well, but she knew it was useless now.

She heard more yelling and excited chatter from the tunnel

behind her, and it was growing louder. It was still a distance away, but closer than she would have liked. Still the tunnel went on, and even when she shone the light from her phone ahead every now and again, hoping to catch sight of the end, the way forward just extended out like a never-ending path.

Her muscles ached and the lack of air also made things difficult. Outside, in the woods, she could suck in as much of it as her body needed, but down here, under layers and layers of earth, it was more difficult.

She tried to push herself on as quickly as she could, but Ashley was also mindful of what could be waiting at the other end. She knew things wouldn't be straight forward. After all, they had been wanting to bring her down here themselves, so it obviously didn't lead to civilisation or a place where help would be waiting.

Once out of the narrow passageway, she knew there would still be work to do.

Someone else was down here. Someone the Webb family spoke of with fear and reverence.

Grandpa.

Ashley had no idea what to expect from him, so there was no real way to prepare herself. She just knew that she needed to be alert and ready to act. The knife Kim had gifted her may not do any good when all was said and done, but Ashley was glad to have a weapon all the same.

The voices were beginning to grow steadily louder, and closer, and her breathing had turned short and shallow. She tried to keep calm and move faster, working her arms and legs as hard as she could, trying to keep everything in a steady rhythm.

The tunnel ahead then began to close up, threatening to block off the way ahead. Ashley felt an increasing sense of claustrophobia as the walls closed in the farther she crawled.

Was it a dead end?

She had visions of getting stuck and being able to do nothing but wait until the family reached her and flayed her.

Thankfully, almost as soon as it had narrowed, the tunnel soon began to open up again, allowing her to crawl faster.

Then, as she checked up ahead again with the light, she saw it; an end to the never ending. The end of this fucking tunnel.

Ashley could see the space open out, but also a steady blue glow that grew a little brighter the closer she got to the end. She wasn't sure of the source of the light, but she didn't care.

She flicked the light off from her phone, not wanting to draw the attention of anyone who may be ahead.

She used the strange glow at the end of the tunnel as her guiding light; a point of focus to press on towards. The stings and scrapes of stone and rock against her skin, and the poke of the blade into her flesh, now mattered little. In fact, they motivated her more. Ashley worked her body quickly, pushing harder and harder.

Soon, she was out, through the opening, and into a staggeringly large space.

It didn't take her long to realise she was in a huge underground cave system of some kind. Stalagmites rose up from the ground, and stalactites dropped from the rocky ceiling above. Looking up, Ashley found the source of the blue glow she had seen from the tunnel.

The entirety of the rock ceiling above was lined with thin, rope-like objects that hung down. The writhing things gave off a fluorescent glow, and there were so many that they acted as a light source. The worm-like creatures were not still; they moved, slowly, twisting and curling.

There were thousands upon thousands of them.

Ashley couldn't be sure what they were, and they initially looked alien to her. The unnatural hue they radiated gave the cave an otherworldly feel.

An idea as to what they might be soon popped into her head: glowworms.

Ashley was still aware of the approaching danger from behind, and saw a clear way forward, a wide pathway that funnelled between the large rock formations and stalagmites that sprung from the ground.

In different circumstances, the whole area could have been considered quite striking and beautiful, if a little oppressive. Right now, though, it was dangerous. On top of that, the thought of one of those worms above dropping down onto her caused goosebumps to crawl along her flesh.

She shook off the notion and began to run forward, following the only trail she could. Hopefully, it would keep going and led to a way out.

If it didn't, and there was no other exit, Ashley was going to be stuck down here with them. And, as big as this place seemed, she couldn't hide forever.

As she ran, a sound caught her attention.

Though it wasn't quite clear enough to pinpoint or recognise, Ashley could have sworn it sounded like a whisper.

Impossible.

She had to keep going and not get distracted. Not let her mind run away with itself. She needed to keep her wits about her.

The she heard it again, clearer this time.

Now there was no doubt.

It was a whisper, and it formed a word she recognised.

The whisper had called her name.

Ashley.

She stopped dead, listening intently, her blood running cold. The words seemed to come from everywhere, and nowhere, at the same time.

She could hear her pursuers growing in volume from behind; their sounds were starting to echo around the stone surface of the cave. But she tried to hear beyond that.

Ashley, it said again.

'Who's there?' she asked out loud, disappointed at herself for the fear she heard in her own voice. After all she had been through, what did she really have to be scared of anymore?

Yet she *was* scared.

Terrified.

Something about all of it just felt wrong, worse than what she had encountered up above with those cannibals. She couldn't explain it, but she could feel a profound sense of dread creeping its way up from her gut, spreading its icy tendrils through her body.

However she also knew that, regardless of whatever was down here, she needed to keep going. Standing here wasn't going to help her in the slightest.

Again she began to run, determined not to stop again unless she was physically made to. She heard that whisper again and couldn't be sure where it was coming from, but ignored it as best she could.

The single word the voice uttered carried weight and menace with it. Hearing it set off waves of foreboding and unease inside of her.

Then something clicked.

There was a reason Ashley couldn't pinpoint where the sound was coming from. It was because it wasn't coming from anywhere.

Not really.

She had been hearing it inside her own head.

Already terrified for her life, the realisation that something was in her head scared Ashley on a new level. Had her mind snapped? Was she crazy?

If not, then what in the hell was speaking to her?

Another sound, but no longer a whisper, this time a mad tittering. It was like nothing she'd ever heard before.

This can't be real, she thought to herself. *It's happened. My mind broke. This isn't real.*

To her horror, she received a response to her own thoughts.

It is very real.

More mocking laughter as she ran, growing louder and louder and impossible to ignore. Ashley wanted to clamp her hands over her ears to drown it out, but knew that would do no good.

'There she is,' she heard another voice call, this one very much real and outside of her own mind. It was a voice she could place too.

It was Ted.

As she rounded a large boulder, she looked back and saw him sprinting towards her. He had closed on her quicker than expected.

The escape, it seemed, was over. Potentially so close to freedom, too.

No escape for you, little thing. You stay here with me.

Ashley's heart was beating faster than she thought was possible. She felt her legs wobble as she ran.

Keep going, keep going, keep going, she thought to herself.

Yes, keep coming. Come see me, lowly thing.

She tried to ignore it and concentrated purely on pushing forward.

As she sprinted round another curve in the path, she saw it.

Ashley stopped dead.

The thing up ahead was impossible. Something so horrific that her mind struggled to process it.

It wasn't of this world.

Couldn't be.

But Ashley knew instantly who this was.

Her voice was shaky as she spoke, unable to hide her fear. 'Grandpa?'

The thing smiled at her. She saw that it had too many teeth for its mouth.

33

It made no sense, this thing before her.

It couldn't be human, at least not anymore, but Ashley got the vague impression that perhaps it once was.

Its form was still vaguely human-like, though somehow it had completely melded into a large expanse of rock.

No, that wasn't right. The wall this thing was fused to was not rock, at least not the same as the rest of the cave. It was black and wet, with small, thin, white veins running from the thing to the wall's outer reaches. The black surface slowly moved and pulsed.

The form at the centre of it all, the thing smiling at her, was of roughly humanoid shape, but its head, and most of its body, had been painfully elongated and twisted, partially melted into a deformed shape. Its bloated, yellowed skin was split and torn, revealing blackened insides beneath. The face still had a mouth, one that was the full width of the head, and it had large sockets that may or may not have contained eyes. One corner of its top lip curled up, giving the mouth a natural scowl, but kept going and met an opening where a nose should have been. A feature she had seen on others in the Webb family.

The monster's torso was unnaturally long and thin, and its ribcage actually sat outside of the skin. Arms splayed out to its side, but instead of hands, the arms ended with writhing tendrils that broke off at the wrists. Its waist simply sunk back into the pulsating wall behind, hiding its lower half.

There was another detail that horrified Ashley as well. Though the large eye sockets were sunken so deeply that what lay beneath was lost to their depths, the thing did have eyes, of a sort. Small, dirty yellow orbs with black pupils lined the length of its body in no definable pattern. Each of them rolled and moved of their own accord, taking in different parts of the surroundings.

Most of these grotesque eyes were now locked on to Ashley.

She noticed something else too. Thin, glistening tubes of flesh ran from the pulsating wall that entombed this thing and up to the ceiling of the cave above, getting lost between the wriggling worms that hung down. From within these translucent tubes, Ashley could see a trickle of crimson liquid working its way down towards the being. It dawned on her that they must have been directly beneath the room where Craig was killed, and she now knew where that stone table was draining the blood to.

Ashley, it said again, still inside her head. Its next words, however, were spoken physically, through a mouth that struggled to form the words.

'*Pretty,*' it said, its voice a strained growl. With its misshapen mouth and lack of lips, enunciating each syllable wasn't easily accomplished. '*I. Will. Claim. You.*'

It heaved out an excited, wheezing chuckle.

The being was far beyond Ashley's understanding of the world, or of the universe. More so than encountering the seemingly inhuman Webb family, seeing this thing shattered what she thought she knew about how things were, and how things were supposed to be.

Her mind reeled.

Then she remembered the knife. But the idea of using it against that thing just seemed absurd. Like sticking a rhino with a pin.

Ashley didn't hear Ted run up behind her and was only aware of him when he lunged into her, tackling her to the ground. She landed face first and struggled to adjust herself. Not to fight him off, but, for reasons she couldn't comprehend, she needed to get herself into a position to look upon the thing that so repulsed her.

'*A. New. Child,*' it said.

'What... what is that?' Ashley stammered out.

'That,' Ted said from on top of her as he pulled her arms behind her back, 'is Grandpa. Say hello.'

'It... it isn't human. It can't be real. It can't be real.'

Footsteps grew louder from behind and Ashley became aware of others joining them. Henry panted as he reached them, his mother just ahead. Ashley heard a gurgling and spluttering as the father, Benjamin, also followed behind, still spitting blood, and still gripping his oozing throat.

The blood seemed darker now.

Tim was nowhere to be seen.

'What took you?' Ted whispered to his mother.

'Henry got himself stuck in the tunnel,' she whispered back. 'It wasn't easy pushing him through.'

Ashley was barely taking in any of this, still looking at the abomination before her. She was then hoisted to her feet by Ted.

'She got away from us, Grandpa,' Ted said, as if answering a question. One Ashley hadn't heard being asked. 'We were going to bring her down to see you, but something happened and she got ahead of us.'

'I know that,' the mother said respectfully. Again, as if in response to something. 'It was a mistake. She should never have been down here on her own.'

A pause. Then Ted again; 'It was his fault,' he said, pointing to Benjamin, who was now down on one knee, looking like he was in absolute agony, like he was about to pass out. 'A girl got the better of him, did that to his throat, which let this one get ahead of us.'

Another pause, then Benjamin tried to say something. It was a gurgling mess and blood spluttered from his mouth.

Ashley realised that there was some kind of conversation going on she was not party to. And after the way that thing had spoken to her inside her head before, she knew exactly how it was taking place.

'Yes,' Adela answered, looking over to her husband. *If he were actually her husband*, Ashley now thought. 'It's true. It's his fault this happened. And because of him, we only had one body to feed on. The other girl is dead, and the meat and blood will soon be too cold. Not enough time to make use of her.'

The smile that seemed a permanent fixture on the thing's hideous face faltered, then fell. It took on a seething quality, though Ashley wasn't quite sure how she deduced that. It was more a feeling that the thing gave off, something it radiated.

Benjamin pulled himself to his feet and began to gurgle incomprehensible words again, this time with more urgency. Ashley couldn't be certain, but it seemed like he was trying to give some kind of apology. He had one bloodied hand held out before him in supplication.

The thing in the wall began to breathe heavily, pushing out its skeletal chest. All of the small eyes on its body rolled in the same direction to focus on Benjamin, who continued to plead in gibberish.

Ashley felt something change in the air around her, as if it somehow became charged with power.

Something was happening.

The rest of the family were looking at Benjamin with an expression she hadn't seen from them before.

Fear.

And soon she saw why.

As Benjamin uselessly tried to reason and beg for his life, Ashley saw his skin slowly begin to change. It was almost unnoticeable at first, but soon it became clearer. Small, black marks began to form on the surface, marks that started to grow and redden in the centre. Then, a familiar smell began to drift towards Ashley, one that reminded her of barbecues on a summer day.

Cooking meat.

Smoke began to rise from the growing, dark patches, and finally Benjamin seemed to realise what was happening. His eyes widened in horror and he shook his head frantically. All of the creature's eyes bore down intensely on Benjamin and, suddenly, he began to shriek in pain.

He dropped to his knees and his skin began to bubble and blister, crisping before Ashley's eyes. Though there was no visible heat source, there was no mistaking what was happening; he was being burned alive.

The man continued to scream as the black and red blisters grew and completely covered him, scorching him, stripping him of his hair.

Soon he was unrecognisable as he rolled around desperately on the floor, the entire expanse of skin now nothing more than bubbling, burnt flesh. The horrific sight, coupled with the smell of cooking meat, was enough to make Ashley gag and dry heave.

Still, Benjamin suffered. Despite all he had done, Ashley actually felt a small amount of pity for him and just wanted the obvious torture to end.

Rather than end, the suffering went on. Benjamin's melting, wax-like skin sloughed from his bones, dropping to the floor.

Eventually, thankfully, his pathetic screams, which had turned into high-pitched squeals, fell away, and Benjamin stopped moving. What remained was a smoking black and red body, mostly stripped of its flesh.

The family all looked down, subdued and scared.

Ashley had begun to assume, after all she had seen, that this family could not die, that somehow they could defy nature and just keep on going and going. Now, she knew, that was not the case. The very thing that seemed to give them their longevity and resilience could very easily strip it away. The man who had once acted as the patriarch to the family was now dead.

She looked back to the beast that had somehow caused such destruction. She saw its deep breathing begin to ease, and the eyes all swivelled away in different directions once more.

Any remaining hope she had of escaping was extinguished in that moment. Battling against seemingly unkillable cannibals was one thing, and it had been hard enough to keep fighting them with any kind of belief she would survive. But seeing the thing down here, Grandpa, something that was even more of an impossibility than the Webb family, kill one of them in such a way...

What chance did that give her?

None, she heard a raspy voice say in her head.

Some of the thing's eyes looked directly at her, and once again the vile abomination formed a twisted smile.

Then its mouth opened.

The family stood in silent shock, unmoving. Henry kept glancing at his now dead father. Though he was a literal giant, he looked like a terrified child. Ashley understood why. Up above ground, where the Webb's only had to deal with people like her, people who were food, they were in charge. They were powerful. They could be hurt, sure, but they would survive. Down here, with this thing, with *Grandpa*, they knew that they could be killed, at any time, and with horrifying ease.

Finally, Adela spoke. 'We're sorry,' she said, her voice quivering. 'Won't let anything like this happen again.' She then paused, as if listening to an unheard sound, and nodded. 'Yes, I understand. We'll make sure we get more, and quick. No matter what. We'll get you food. We'll send Tim back out as soon as we're done.'

'*No,*' it said, this time physically. '*Her.*'

All eyes fell on Ashley.

'Really?' asked Ted, still holding Ashley. 'Is she to be turned?'

'*Yes,*' it said. The thin tendrils at the end of its wrists began to wriggle and writhe, almost excitedly.

Ashley heard Ted let out a small laugh. 'I knew you would like her, Grandpa.'

It was a stupid thing to think about, given the situation, but it seemed so odd that they called it that. *Grandpa*? It wasn't human, so why give it some kind of family connotation. And, given how this family seemed to grow and add members, she had half an idea that none of these people were actually related. Not by blood.

Clever girl, the thing said to her, and only her. It was again in her head. *The family connects through my bloodline, not their own. Blood that will soon fill your veins. When that happens, you will give yourself over to me. You will be mine forever. A mere puppet for me to toy with. And you will thank me for it.*

'What are you?' Ashley asked again, gritting her teeth. If she was going to be turned into one of these cannibals, then she at least wanted to know what this thing was.

The thing, it seemed, decided to humour her.

Noting you can understand. The body you see before you is the remnant of the first man who found me down here. He could not comprehend me, your kind never can, not fully, so I took him as my host. His son was with him. He was the second, and he now lies on the ground beside you, stripped of his flesh. He was the first of my servants, and though he is of no more use to me now, he brought me more of you meat puppets to control. In return, I granted them certain gifts.

'Why?' Ashley asked. 'Why do you need this?'

My existence in this place is not without effort, and for that I need sustenance. The family gathers the food we all need to go on.

Ashley noted the term; *existence in this place*?

She didn't think it was referring to this cave.

'A family this big seems overkill just to bring you sacrifices.'

A pack of dogs will defend their master much more effectively than a single hound. My pets serve me well... usually. Until now. Until you.

'So where do you come from?' Ashley asked. 'Where are you from?'

A place of chaos. A place of horror. And of desecration and torment.

'Hell?' Ashley asked. The word spilled from her mouth before she had a chance to consider the absurdity of it. Then again, the situation she was in was far beyond absurd, anyway. Was it really such a stretch?

There is no such place. Hell is just a term. The place I am from is very real and full of horrors that would break your small mind. Things exist there that you could not understand. But once I turn you, I will open the door a little, and you will gain some small measure of true knowledge.

'I won't let you,' Ashley said, trying to back up. Ted held her firm. 'I'll die first.'

Only if I allow it.

Then the abomination opened its mouth again and physically spoke to its family.

'Bring. Her. To. Me.'

34

Ashley fought against Ted, but it was in vain; the man that held her was just too strong. Against her will, she was forced forward, ever closer to that grotesque thing.

'Let me go,' she screamed, trying to dig the heels of her boots into the ground to halt her progress. Ted simply pushed her harder.

'Don't fight it,' he said, 'it'll hurt much less if you just let it happen.'

The idea of letting this happen to her, of them having their way with her, of becoming one of them and doing the things they did, sickened her. She couldn't let it happen.

Ashley knew now that survival was just not possible. And she didn't count becoming one of these monsters as true survival. That wasn't survival, it was submission.

And it was not an option.

The only way to truly save herself was to choose death. If she were dead, then they could do what they wanted with her husk of a body, but she would be free of them, somewhere where they couldn't touch her.

The otherworldly thing before her slowly drew one of its

arms out of the pulsing wall, holding out the long appendage before her. She saw the thin, snakelike tendrils all had small mouths, or suckers, that puckered at the air. Dark liquid began to ooze from these mouths, dripping to the floor.

Grandpa's blood.

She knew it intended to infuse her with its blood—that was how she would be turned—and she was forced closer to the wriggling things as they wormed their way towards her mouth.

Desperate, Ashley let her legs go limp and tried to drop to the floor. Ted still held her arms, which were twisted behind her back, and when she dropped she felt a sharp pain in her wrists and shoulders as they strained against her body weight.

Ted then pulled at her arms, trying to hoist her back up, increasing the pain as he did. Ashley refused to budge, flopping like a puppet with its strings cut, or like a disobedient child who did not want to be held.

'Fucking move,' Ted said, trying to push her forward, but Ashley just flopped farther to the floor. Ted had to adjust himself and grab at her shoulder to keep her from falling face first. He then stepped ahead of her and began to drag her forward, again by her arms.

'Silly games like this won't work,' Ted said.

Ashley felt like her shoulders were about to dislocate, but she welcomed the pain. It was a sign of her struggle, something she could cling to.

'Now stop fucking around,' he yelled, exploding in anger. It seemed he was a little embarrassed to be seen having so much trouble with her in front of Grandpa. He stepped towards her, grabbed Ashley's hair, and raised a hand to slap her around the head, releasing one of her wrists.

'Fuck you,' Ashley said, her body still a dead weight. He hit her, the blow powerful enough to dizzy her, but through it all Ashley kept her focus and worked her free hand behind her back.

'Fine,' Ted said and spat at her, 'I'll carry you, if I need to.'

He released her other arm and reached down for her body, ready to grab her and lift her up, but Ashley's hand found what it was looking for.

She pulled the knife free from the back of her trousers. With a scream, she thrust it upwards, remembering how Kim had fought off the now dead father, and aimed directly for Ted's throat.

Ted's eyes opened wide in shock and he let out a gasp as the knife plunged into his neck. Everything seemed to pause. Blood pooled around the protruding steel and ran down its length and down his throat. No one moved in that instant, clearly surprised at her actions.

At her resolve.

Ashley then took the handle in both hands and yanked sideways as hard as she could.

Red liquid slopped from the yawning wound she had opened up, and it coated her chest. Ted instinctively brought up his hand, but the gash was so deep that his fingers sunk inside, getting lost to the knuckle. Blood ran from his mouth and he fell sideways.

She knew he wasn't dead, but at least he was down.

Then, however, the shock began to wear off of the family.

'Get her,' Adela screamed.

Ashley sprang up to her feet and held the weapon out

before her as Henry boomed forward. She backed up, and an idea formed in her mind. One that would cost her her life, but would ensure she would not become one of these things.

She turned her back to the approaching Henry and ran in a different direction.

Towards the thing in the wall.

Towards dear old Grandpa.

'What's she doing?' the mother yelled, frantic. Ashley ducked under the thing's outstretched arm, feeling the writhing tendrils snap and drool at her back, and thrust the knife forward, throwing her body weight behind the attack. The knife ricocheted off the edge of an eye socket, striking bone, and found its way completely inside of it with a squelch. She pushed hard and buried it up to the hilt.

Again, everyone froze. She expected some kind of reaction, some kind of screams or roars of anger from the family or from the thing, but there was nothing. The family didn't know what to do, and the thing didn't seem to be affected by the knife protruding from its head. It moved its arm back towards Ashley, and again she ducked, pulling herself back and drawing the knife with her. She managed to scramble away just as the arm tried to take hold of her.

Looking at the steel of the blade, she saw it was coated in a dark, almost black substance, one a little too thick to be blood.

Silly girl, the thing called to her, mocking her, from inside her own head. *I cannot die. But you can.*

'I welcome it,' she said. 'I won't become a monster.'

So be it.

'*Kill. Her,*' it said aloud to the family.

Ted tried to get to his feet, but he was struggling to stand, still preoccupied with his open throat, but Henry and his mother started to advance. Ashley held the bloodied knife out to ward them off and looked past them, seeing the path back towards the tunnel.

They were going to kill her, that much was certain. It was what she wanted, but that path was a potential way out. Did she really have to just lay down and accept death?

Could she actually fight her way through and get free?

The giant and his mother slowly stalked towards her, closing the gap, but evidently wary of her.

Showing her a grudging respect.

Ashley assessed the situation. Out of the two of them, given Henry's mass and bulk, she guessed Adela would be the faster of them, so if it came down to a direct foot race, she would have a better chance against Henry. Which meant she needed to take out the mother, or at least slow her down.

She twisted the knife in her grip, taking the tip of the blade in two fingers of her stronger right hand. She had no idea if what she was planning would work, but what did she have to lose? Ashley pulled her right arm back and held her left out before her, both to aim and to balance herself. She then flung her right arm forward and launched the knife toward Adela.

Ashley's heart was in her mouth as the blade spiralled through the air towards its target.

She half expected to see it sail past the old woman and fall harmlessly to the floor, but it didn't. After all the shitty luck she and her friends had suffered this weekend, it seemed some was finally on her side. The knife found its target, blade first, and Ashley heard the wet *thunk* as it squelched into the woman's stomach. Adela let out a cry of pain and dropped to all fours.

Ashley heard that thing in her head again, seemingly

amused by everything.

Very good, little girl. You have a gift for this. A shame that you cannot be one of my pets. You would have excelled. And you would have learned such wonderful truths.

'Ma,' Henry screamed and ran to Adela.

Ashley set off, waiting around no longer, but quickly cast a glance back to the thing in the wall. She saw that it was again breathing deeply, and all of its beady little eyes were looking at her.

She felt it again, that charge in the air.

'I'm fine,' Adela wheezed out as Ashley sprinted past her and her giant son.

As she ran, she began to smell it. Faint at first, then more potent.

Cooking meat.

Then the pain struck. Ashley held up her hands and saw that the skin had started to blacken.

She remembered what had happened to Benjamin, only moments ago, and realised her fate.

She was to be burned alive.

35

Ashley screamed in agony as the sizzling pain began to spread.

This is going to hurt, the thing taunted. *Stay still and accept your fate, and the pain will be much less. That I promise you.*

Adela was still coughing on the floor, but motioned to Henry. 'Get her,' she groaned, waving her arms.

Ashley ran.

She couldn't avoid the agonising death that had already begun. She knew the meat would cook and fall from her bones and she would be alive to feel it, as Benjamin had been, and that terrified her. But she was too scared to stop and simply let that agonising end just happen to her.

So she ran, sprinted for all she was worth, because there was nothing else to be done. She pumped her legs as hard and fast as she could. Through it all, the hot pain grew worse and seared and boiled through her. She screamed as she ran, seeing blisters form on the back of her hands and arms.

Come back, you bitch. You fucking cunt.

The thing sounded angry, furious even. But more than that, Ashley was sure there was a hint of desperation.

She heard Henry's heavy footfalls behind her as he gave a laboured chase.

The pain was like a hot lava rolling over her flesh.

She continued to sprint.

The smell of her own burning skin grew stronger and turned her stomach.

This is it, she thought as she ran around a large rock formation, out of view of that horrible thing, readying herself for the worst of it. *I'm going to die.*

Return to me, you pathetic husk. Do it now and I may yet let you live.

She ignored the empty promise. Thoughts of seeing Benjamin's skin melt and hang from his body were fresh in her mind, and she knew she could expect the same excruciating end, but all she could do was focus on the exertion of running and hope it could block out some of the pain.

For a little while, at least.

Up ahead, illuminated by the writhing, glowing worms from the ceiling, she saw a dark opening in the rock wall; the opening to the tunnel. As she ran towards it, Ashley briefly wondered if those glowworms were just a natural phenomenon, or if they were somehow related to that thing that was now burning her alive.

She was quickly through the hole and into the tunnel, jumping down to all fours and scrambling forward, before she realised something.

The searing pain that had been building and building was no more. Well, that was wrong, the pain was still very much there, but it didn't seem to be getting any worse. Ashley didn't want to stop to check herself over, as there wasn't time for that; she could still hear Henry running after her. In fact, she soon heard him enter the tunnel behind her, but she was almost certain that whatever was starting to happen to her had stopped.

The burning smell had faded and, she noted, the voice was no longer with her. The monster's taunts and demands had ceased. She tried to look down at her hands as she crawled, to see if the black patches and blisters, blisters she could still feel, were still spreading, but it was just too dark.

Could it be? Could she let herself believe that maybe she had gotten free of the abomination's influence?

Again, she thought back to what had happened to Benjamin, and she remembered how the thing in the wall had acted when it ended him. It had started to breathe heavily, as if exerting intense concentration or strain, but she also remembered that all of its horrible little eyes had spun to lock directly onto him.

And maybe that was the key.

When she ran around the rock formation, she had broken its line of sight, and hopefully also broken whatever link or ability it had to scorch her from this earth. Perhaps she had cleared its range?

Perhaps there was hope?

But that hope was precarious, because even now she heard Henry thundering through the tunnel behind her.

How can anyone that big move so fast?

'You're going to be sorry for that,' he shouted, his voice sounding close. 'You stabbed Ma, and I'm going to make you sorry for that. I'm going to twist your head off like I did with your friend.'

Up ahead, Ashley felt the tunnel close in, and she remembered the section from earlier. Things were going to get a little tighter.

If she could just keep going, perhaps Henry would be slowed down, giving her a chance to get farther away.

She pushed herself through and, just as she was about to give an extra burst of speed, she heard Henry roar from behind. The sound startled her because it was so close, closer than she thought he'd been to her. Ashley spun her head and could just make out Henry's form in the darkness, almost upon her.

A large hand thrust out and grabbed her ankle.

'Gotcha,' he said. She heard him groan as he slowly squeezed himself forward. The pain in her ankle from his grip was immense, like the bone was actually being crushed in his hand. He grunted again and Ashley realised they were sounds of exertion as he was trying to push himself through the narrowing gap. It would have been the ideal time to put some distance between them, but he had hold of her tight.

She was going nowhere.

Unless...

Without thinking, or really caring anymore, Ashley acted. Instead of pulling away from Henry, as he would have expected, she twisted herself in the tunnel and lunged herself forward towards his bulk. She heard a surprised grunt as the hand released from her leg and grabbed at her waist. Ashley fell into him, face to face, feeling his breath on her. It made her gag.

'Decided to give up? Well, too late, I'm not going to go easy on you.' His grip tightened, squeezing her waist. 'I'm going to make this hurt. Going to pull your arms and legs off, make you suffer like the insect you are. In fact, I'm gonna—'

He stopped his taunting and began to scream.

Ashley did not wait around to listen to him any longer. While he had been letting her know what he was going to do, she had already acted and brought her hands up to his fat face. His rubbery skin was sweaty, but her hands felt their way into position, and she plunged her thumbs into his eyes, as hard as she could.

As her appendages pressed into his eyeballs, Henry shrieked and howled and brought up a big arm to swat her away. Ashley expected it and pulled her thumbs free, ducking down. His large arm sailed over her, and she was quickly up again, continuing her attack, again burying her thumbs, digging the nails in first, into his beady eyes. The first time she had felt a resistance, this time she felt a gooey pop.

Warm liquid ran down the heels of her hands. Ashley screamed in anger, in absolute fury, and pushed harder and harder, letting out every bit of pent-up aggression that had, so far, been repressed by fear.

Henry's hands rose again, but she had done what she needed to. She quickly turned and scampered away as the large, grotesque monster continued to howl.

Through his screams, Ashley heard another voice grow close. It was Adela, the mother, and she was yelling at her son, telling him to move. Henry just continued his childlike wails.

'I can't get by you,' Adela screamed at Henry, 'and she's getting away!'

And so she was.

Ashley crawled as fast as she could up the tunnel, much faster than she had on her descent, renewed by an adrenaline rush borne from genuine hope. Against all odds, she knew she had a chance at escape.

On and on she went, pushing up the incline, forcing her muscles to work harder for her. Soon, she saw a dull light source in the ceiling up ahead, one that lit the end of the tunnel.

It was the hole Kim had pushed her down earlier.

Ashley crawled to the light and looked up. The heavy, metal grate was open, bent into an odd shape. She took a moment to steady herself, got to her feet, and jumped, managing to grab onto the lip of the opening. She used her legs to give herself purchase against the dirt wall and, with great effort, pulled herself up, back into that room of desecration.

It was horrifying to once again see what had become of Craig, but Ashley stopped dead in her tracks when she saw poor Kim's headless body sprawled out on the floor. An enormous pool of blood nestled at the torn and bloodied stump of her neck.

Ashley then slowly walked through the room, trying to keep her eyes forward, not wanting to look at what had become of her friends. Especially Kim, who had given her life for Ashley.

As well as ripping Kim's head from her body, the family had evidently decided to feed on her as well. Her coat had been removed, piled next to her body, and patches of skin were savagely torn away. Her stomach, too, had been pulled open.

The thought of leaving Kim's body there in such a state didn't sit well with Ashley, but what else could she do?

An idea struck her, but she would have to be quick. Maybe she couldn't get Kim out of there, but she could at least bring back something her friend valued. She would make sure that one item didn't stay here in this hell with these things.

Ashley squatted next to her friend, but looked away, not wanting to see too much. It was a mistake, though, and she pulled in a disgusted gasp. She had turned her gaze to the side, but only succeed in seeing Kim's dismembered head in the corner. It lay on its side, eyes wide in horror, mouth open.

Like it was mid scream.

It looked both real and like a cheap dummy at the same time.

'I'm sorry,' Ashley whispered and dug through the pockets of the coat, quickly finding what she was looking for; the gold lighter left to Kim by her mother.

Ashley put it in her own pocket and got back to her feet. She couldn't hear anyone else approaching through the tunnel, but knew she still needed to be quick. She set off running again, up the stone steps, back to the basement. While the hanging bodies of victims past was still a macabre and gruesome sight, given what Ashley had just escaped, it felt like a step closer to sanity.

A step back towards the real world and out of this nightmare.

She ran past the hanging meat and bones as carefully as she could and took the timber steps two at a time back up to the kitchen, back up to the main level of the house.

She paused for breath, leaning against a wall in the hallway. Soon she would leave this place behind, forever.

But before she did, an idea grew in her mind, worming its way to the surface.

An idea of how she could get revenge on these people.

Leaving the place standing, after what had happened, not just tonight, but over who knows how many years, seemed wrong.

These fuckers, what was left of them, shouldn't get to just carry on. Something had to be done. And she had an idea of what that could be. She had seen one of them die. And how had it happened?

Fire.

That, and some horrific, impossible being that had abilities she couldn't comprehend. But what if fire was the key to it? What if that was the element that could actually hurt them? She remembered how Tim had always been afraid of fire and the story he had told as to why. Clearly a lie used to build sympathy, but what if the fear was real?

The jigsaw pieces fell into place.

Her mind was made up, now driven more for revenge for her friends than to save her own life.

Ashley would scorch the place from the earth.

Working quickly, she retrieved Kim's mother's lighter. The kitchen was littered with junk, some of which were old rags of clothing; rags which were quite dry. She held the lighter to the bits of cloth until a flame took hold. Then she did the same again and again to whatever else she could find that was flammable.

Small pockets of fire began to grow, but she needed more, and there was another room she knew would be a good place to go next.

The library.

A room they had investigated earlier, back before their nightmare had started in earnest.

It seemed like a lifetime ago now, not just a few hours.

She ran to that room and again got to work with the lighter, getting most of the books and loose sheets of paper to take quite easily. However, as she worked, a particular book caught her eye. For the first time in a while, Ashley thought ahead, to what she would do if she actually made it back to civilisation.

She would need to tell the police about what had

happened. Her friends were dead, not something she could ignore, but how was she supposed to explain it all?

She picked up the leather-bound book, which had been sitting on the small writing table, and quickly skimmed through some of the pages. Flames danced their way around the shelves, crawling over the wood and books like liquid, but that did not impede her concentration. Ashley quickly realised the book was a kind of journal, written by Benjamin. She saw passages mentioning other places not of this earth, and there were sketches of things that were absolutely not human; one of which she recognised.

A crudely sketched rendition of the thing below the ground.

Grandpa.

The rapidly spreading fire begin to give off a strong heat, and Ashley knew she had to go. She tucked the book under her arm and ran outside, onto the porch, into the night air.

Into freedom.

Almost.

As she broke free of the threshold, a fist swung from beside the door and caught her hard on the side of the chin.

The force of the blow shook her jaw and rattled her teeth, and she fell sideways to the porch floor. The book spilled from her grasp and she rolled to her back, dazed and disorientated.

Tim looked down at her, his mouth smeared with blood.

'Hello, little mouse.'

36

Tim couldn't believe it.

Surely it was impossible.

No one had ever returned from seeing Grandpa, at least not as the same person they were before going down.

Mother, Ted, and Henry had all gone down there after her, and even Father had followed, in his pathetic state, clutching at his neck. She had been outnumbered by things infinitely superior and stronger than her.

So how was it she was able to escape?

And her, of all people?

The fucking mouse?

It was insanity.

After Mother had ordered them all down after her, Tim had hung back. He'd made as if to follow, but after she dropped down, he simply waited. They were all too distracted to notice he wasn't with them.

And besides, he knew he only needed a little time.

The food left in that room would soon spoil, and Tim was not a fan of waste, so leaving it was a crime. He had approached Kim's headless body.

And started to feed.

At first, he just wanted a small amount, just enough to fill him a little. More than the meagre scraps he'd been given.

But as he tasted the succulent, salty flesh, he couldn't stop. The hunger, the desire to feed, had taken over.

So, he got to work.

Tim didn't care if they all came back and found him like this. Fuck them, he'd waited long enough for what he was owed and was tired of being on the fringe.

He was one of them, one of Grandpa's children just as much as the rest were, and as far as Tim was concerned, that meant getting what was promised.

No more waiting.

He gorged.

And had kept going until he heard commotion in the tunnel.

The noise, which sounded like Henry and Mother, snapped him back to reality. They would find him and see he had disobeyed them.

He remembered Father's threat of a trip down to see Grandpa.

Fear of what that meant, and what would become of him, forced him to flee, and he ran from the house, hoping to give them time to calm down.

He hadn't eaten enough to change him, hopefully, so there was no need to overreact. He could still do his job, just as he always had.

So, he hid in the trees.

Watching.

Waiting.

Then, Tim saw something he couldn't quite believe.

Ashley, the little mouse girl, was free. And, judging by her actions as she set fire to Father's books, she had clearly not been turned.

But at the same time, she wasn't her old self, not the doormat Tim knew.

She looked full of anger and hate and... purpose.

He couldn't even begin to comprehend how she had gotten away, but he saw an opportunity, an opportunity to prove himself again to the family, make them forget, or not even notice, what he'd done. He would capture her, the girl who had obviously given them the slip, and prove he deserved to be among them. Not as a little worker ant, but shoulder to shoulder as an equal.

He slowly made his way to the doorway, hiding just beside the frame, and ducked below the window to the library. He pressed his back against the wall and waited.

He knew, eventually, he would have to deal with the fire the girl was starting, and that was something he did not look forward to, but first he needed to deal with her.

He didn't want to just run in and attack her. Tim didn't know how, but Ashley was up here and the family weren't. They were nowhere to be seen. He didn't know how that was possible, but there it was, so he knew he needed to afford her some respect. At least until he could figure out what kind of threat she realistically posed.

He waited a little longer and soon heard her running footsteps make their way down the hall. She ran from the house, oblivious to his presence.

Tim was already poised and let fly with as hard a punch as he could muster. His fist hit its mark.

The feel of the impact was satisfying, as was watching the girl flail to the floor.

That was easy.

He strode over to her and looked down.

'Hello, little mouse,' he said.

37

ASHLEY SAW STARS.

Her vision was spinning, her jaw ached terribly, and she felt a pressure push down on her throat.

Tim had taken his boot and stepped down onto her neck, pinning her to the floor. He bent forward and studied her.

'Where are my family?' he asked. At first, she didn't answer, but he increased the pressure, causing her to gag. 'Where?'

'Still down there,' Ashley said.

'And how did you get away?'

'I ran.'

'Bullshit, I don't believe it. What happened?'

The pressure on Ashley's throat eased a little, allowing her to speak more freely.

'What happened?' she asked. 'You really wanna know? Well, first, that fucking thing down there, your Grandpa, killed your father. Burned him alive.' Tim winced. 'Then I cut your brother's throat. He's still down there, probably gurgling on his own blood. Then I stabbed your mother.

Right in the gut. And to finish? I gouged out that fat fucker's eyes and left him in the tunnel like a stuck pig. That's what happened.'

He was silent for a moment, giving serious thought to her words. 'Bullshit,' he said eventually. 'You couldn't have done all that. No one could have, let alone *you*.'

'Go and see for yourself,' she said. He paused again, looking her over.

'What happened to you? What are those marks? Those burns?'

Ashley had seen the blisters, red and angry, on her skin. Whilst ugly, they hadn't been as bad as she'd feared. However, she had only seen what they had done to her arms and had no idea what state rest of her body was in.

'That fucking monster, it tried to do to me what it did to your father,' she said. 'But I didn't let it'

The fire in the house behind them began to spread. Ashley could hear the flames crackle.

'You're lying,' Tim said through gritted teeth.

'No,' she said, 'I'm not. And you know I'm not, don't you?'

'I don't know what to think,' he said, shaking his head.

'What is that thing down there?' Ashley asked, partly playing for time, partly genuinely curious.

'Grandpa? He's nothing you can understand. Besides, why should I tell you anything?'

'Just curious,' she said. 'Not every day you see something that goes against everything you ever believed in.'

Tim laughed, but he wasn't mocking. 'Yeah, I guess he is something to behold. I remember a similar feeling when I first saw him. Kinda takes your breath away, doesn't he?'

'So, what is he? Things like that don't exist.'

'Well, Father knows more than I do, but apparently Father is dead now, isn't he?'

'Tell me,' Ashley said. 'I need to know.'

Tim shrugged, but went on. 'It was Father who first found it down there. He was with his father at the time. They were mapping out a tunnel they found, or something like that, when they came across... whatever it was. It looked different back then, according to Father, but it took the older man, used his body as its own, and then turned Father. That was the start of it all. Father followed its instructions and found someone else, someone suitable; his wife at the time. She was turned—that would be Mother—and they started to build a family. And we grew from there.'

'But why does it need to do that? What is it?' Ashley asked.

'Hard to explain, I only know what Grandpa showed me. When he turns you, when his old blood works its way into your veins, it shows you things. I don't know if it's deliberate or not, but you get these... visions. The blood in us craves food. Sustenance. So, we oblige, and the more we eat, the more it shows us. About how things really are in the universe. I was never one for learning when I was... like you. Didn't care for it. But let me tell you, the kind of knowledge that thing shows us, it's addictive. We also get stronger the more we feast, but it changes us, too, makes us look different, as you've seen. And, contrary to what you might think, getting people out here isn't easy, especially these days. People go missing nowadays and it's a big thing. The world's a small place, and word gets around quick. So, it isn't easy for us to stay hidden. We don't want too much attention here, and the woods are protected to an extent. Grandpa has made it his domain, and it gives off a certain vibe, for lack of a better term. People just want to avoid the place. Bad in some respects, because we don't get people just wandering though anymore, but it protects us as well.'

'So you have to work for your supper?'

'Yeah, I guess so. Don't judge me, Ashley. I mean, yeah, it turns out being a monster is actually kind of fun. Fuck it, it's more than fun, it's euphoric, but we do it out of necessity. Grandpa's blood is in us and we can't ignore what the blood wants. So, we oblige.'

'But our families will realise we've gone missing,' Ashley said. 'They'll send the police to look for us. People will come.'

Tim shook his head. 'No, they won't. It's a big area outside these woods, a big place to search. There are other pockets of trees and woodland around here, and those places might get searched, but this place? Nope, afraid not. Grandpa's protection is enough. Always has been.'

'And how long have you been doing this?'

'Me? Well, I'm older than I look. A lot older. You wouldn't believe me if I told you. But the family... I guess some of them have been doing it for centuries.'

It sounded impossible to Ashley, but, after all she'd seen, she had no doubt he was telling the truth. 'And you never thought to fight against it? Did you ever think that this was wrong?'

He shook his head. 'Doesn't work that way. Once he's inside you, then that's it. Besides, how can anyone fight something like that? You saw it, didn't you? It can't be fought, Ashley, only obeyed.'

'But you could try,' Ashley said, trying to reason with any kind of humanity he might have left.

'No,' Tim said, as if talking to a child, 'you can't. The longer we go without eating, the worse it gets. The impulses he embeds in us get stronger and harder to control. The violent urges, the aggression, the depravity; those are the things it revels in. The only way to satisfy those urges is to indulge, and that's one of the reasons we do what we do. The longer we go without, the harder it is to control. Fuck, you saw how my family treated each other. Dysfunctional hardly covers it.'

'Try to kill it,' Ashley said.

'You can't.'

'Try.'

'You can't!' he shouted. Tim then turned his head, aware that the flames were getting stronger. She saw a brief look of fear in his eyes.

'Fire,' Ashley said in realisation. 'Fire can hurt you. It can kill you people, can't it?'

'Knowing that isn't going to do you any good, little mouse. Not now.'

'But will it work on that thing?'

'No,' he said. 'I'm not lying when I say it can't be killed, Ashley. Fire has its uses, sure. It can burn away his link to us, his link to our reality, but nothing more.'

'So what would happen if we set it on fire, then? Torched the fucker? Would that send it back to wherever the hell it's from?'

Tim laughed again, genuinely amused. 'Jesus, Ashley, I have to give you credit. I've never seen this side of you before. Never knew you had it in you. Suddenly, you're this kickass warrior girl, huh? I like it, I have to say. But no, you'd never get the chance. He would stop you. And even if you somehow succeeded, fire won't kill it. He would only come back. He is... forever.'

'But we could try, Tim.'

'No,' he said, 'we couldn't. You can't talk me round to this, Ashley. I'd never go against him. And he knows that. Even if I had half a desire to, he's just too strong. The place he's from, it's not like our world, our existence. From what

Father has told me, and from what I've seen, it's like a living nightmare. Sometimes the things that exist there find a doorway through here.' Tim then leaned forward, putting more weight on Ashley's throat. 'And you wanna know the scariest thing?'

'What?' Ashley squeaked out.

'That thing down there, as powerful as he is, he isn't one of the worst. In fact, I think he's pretty low on the food chain where he's from, compared to some of the other things that roam around there. How crazy is that? Can you imagine if one of the really big, nasty ones wanted to find their way here? We'd all be fucked.'

He laughed, but it was a manic laugh, one that belied a genuine fear. Whatever he'd seen, whatever visions he'd been given, as awesome as they might have been, they clearly scared him.

His laughter died down and he looked back at the ever-growing fire.

'So, Grandpa killed Father, huh?'

Ashley nodded as best she could with his boot on her throat. 'Yes.'

'Then that opens up a space,' Tim said, shrugging. 'I thought maybe I'd get my shot if they got rid of Claudia, like they were planning, but this might work as well.'

'No it won't,' Ashley said, struggling against his weight, fighting the urge to gag. 'Do you really think you'll get what you want now? They couldn't get me to join, could they? That means you're fucked. They still need their little errand boy, which means you'll still only get their leftovers.'

The pressure on her throat increased again.

'No,' he said, gritting his teeth in anger. 'Things need to change. And I'll make sure they do.'

Ashley had hit a nerve, goaded him to anger, just as

she'd hoped. Whilst he bubbled with rage, she had brought a leg up and aimed the sole of her boot at Tim. She kicked out, hard, extending her leg with everything she could. The sole of her boot sunk between his legs.

Tim's eyes opened wide and he let out a noise, something between a groan and whimper. He grabbed his crotch, back-pedalled a few steps, and doubled over.

Ashley got to her feet, rubbing her aching throat.

She set herself, then ran towards him with a roar.

38

TIM'S TESTICLES THROBBED, the dull ache making him light-headed and nauseous. The bitch had kicked him so hard she'd almost popped his balls.

Before he knew it, he heard her scream, and she came sprinting at him.

In that moment, he genuinely thought Ashley had lost it.

He could do no more than brace himself as Ashley crashed into him with such force that he was thrown back into the library window. The single pane of glass reverberated and cracked under his weight. Still reeling, Tim barely had time to bring his hands up in defence before Ashley charged him again, tackling him. The glass of the window behind them gave way and they both fell through.

Tim's world spun in a shower of glass and he found himself inside, on the library floor, with Ashley sprawled out beside him. He was also aware of the sudden increase in temperature.

He looked up and saw just how bad the fire had gotten; the room was engulfed in flames. The bookshelves were a blazing inferno, and the fire had even taken hold of the wooden walls at the far end of the room.

No. This can't happen. This can't happen. Not like this.

There wasn't much Tim was genuinely scared of anymore. Though he wasn't as strong as the others in his family, he could still recover from most things, painful though they may be. This, though, would be different. There would be no recovery.

No coming back.

And it would be agonising.

He had to escape.

Tim got to back to his feet, ignoring Ashley who lay, coughing, on the floor, and tried to ignore the pain that still throbbed from his groin. He stumbled back towards the now broken window. Upon taking a step, he felt a sudden stab of pain in his back and yelled out. Tim reached a hand around and felt a shard of glass sticking out from his lower left side, something that must have happened during the fall. He grabbed it and pulled, flaring up more pain, but it refused to budge.

Fuck it, he could deal with that later.

He was aware of Ashley slowly getting to her feet as well, but that didn't matter, he just needed be outside, away from the heat and the smoke and flames. Everything else could wait.

He fell on the sill of the window, feeling some remaining jagged glass press into his stomach, and began to roll through it.

But something stopped him.

A hand, grabbing the belt of his trousers.

He turned to see the bitch, Ashley, holding him, teeth clenched and jaw set. Her face was smattered with light burn marks, her cheek was gashed open, and she was covered in cuts and bruises and filth and dirt, yet she would still not just give up and die.

Warrior girl indeed.

He felt a begrudging respect towards her, but in that moment, respect didn't matter, survival did. His hand wormed around a shard of glass still stuck in the frame. It drew blood as he pulled it free, ready to thrust it into her weak and supple flesh.

As he made to turn his body, the pain from the glass in his back erupted again and, with a scream, he looked down to see Ashley was forcing it deeper inside of him with her free hand.

He coughed and spat blood, lashing out an elbow that knocked her back.

'You fucking bitch,' he screamed. He held up the shard of glass and charged at her, enraged that someone as lowly and weak as her seemed to be destroying everything his family had built.

The glass found nothing but air as Ashley dropped a hip, then weaved the other way, grabbing him tightly around the waist. She pulled at him, using his own momentum against him, and toppled them both into the flame-engulfed bookcase on the far wall. The flames were everywhere now, and Tim felt their stinging heat on him.

'No!' he yelled, trying to pat himself down, not even knowing if the flames had spread to him. It was a reaction he couldn't control. 'No, get it off me.'

He began to scream, aware he was losing it. But he couldn't afford to lose it.

Not now.

If he kept his head, he could still get out. He could still make that bitch suffer for what she'd done.

But the panic that had set in was hard to overcome.

Was this akin to what their victims felt?

He didn't care for the irony.

'Tim,' he heard Ashley yell, and he looked up. She'd moved to the side of the bookcase, pressing herself into it, letting the flames lick and kiss at her, seemingly uncaring. He soon realised what she was doing as the bookcase began to creak. 'Fuck you.'

He looked up and saw the top of the case begin to fall.

Tim tried to run, to scamper and crawl out of the way, desperate to reach safety.

But it was not to be.

A heavy, scalding weight crushed down onto him, pinning him to the floor. It snuffed out any hope of survival.

The bookcase lay on top of him and the fire that coated it so completely now began to find its way to his flesh. It took hold of his clothing first, and he could feel the skin beneath begin to sear as fire did what it did best.

He screamed and squealed in pain.

No, not like this, please. Please, no. Please, please, please.

Tim flattened his hands on the ground and pushed, trying to lift the heavy piece of furniture that weighed down on him. It took a lot of strain, but he managed to get it to raise slightly. If he could just crawl out—

It suddenly dropped heavily again, forcing itself down on him, flattening him to the floor. Twisting his head, he saw that Ashley had planted a foot on the top of it and was pushing down, trapping him. He tried desperately again to lift it, but his arms were pinned tight and he could find no purchase.

The flames began to ravage his body. His clothes now completely took hold and set ablaze. Tim could do nothing but lie there, helpless, and scream as the fire engulfed him completely.

39

It was quite a sight, seeing the man she thought she loved turn into a human torch beneath her.

But he was never really that man. It had all been an act, a way to fool her and her friends. Just to get them out here.

To kill them.

And he'd almost succeeded.

Almost.

Now, Ashley hoped, he was feeling a little of what his victims must have felt.

Helpless, unable to stop the pain inflicted upon him.

Unable to avoid death as his life was slowly taken away.

Tim still screamed and writhed, his cries high-pitched and desperate.

It wasn't a sound she could ever enjoy, because she wasn't like them, she wasn't a monster, but it did bring her some closure, some measure of revenge.

Flames threatened to wrap around the leg she was using to push down on the bookshelf. She'd planted her foot in a small section where the fire hadn't yet taken hold, but that space had dwindled fast and was now almost non-existent.

But even if the fire caught her, she refused to let up. Not until she was sure Tim was dead.

In the time it took for him to stop screaming, and for his melting body to fall still, Ashley never once looked away.

She watched him die.

And when she was certain, absolutely positive that he was dead, she finally removed her foot from the blazing bookshelf. She had cut it fine, too, as the material of her hiking trousers had started to melt and smoulder.

The heat and smoke in the room was becoming unbearable and, now that Tim was finally dead, she needed to turn her attention back on herself.

Back to survival.

She looked once more upon Tim's fire ravaged-body, then vaulted through the window to the porch outside.

The air felt fresh and clean, causing a coughing fit.

Ashley grabbed the book she'd dropped earlier, after Tim had struck her, and ran off into the woods.

40

ASHLEY'S JOURNEY back through the woods was a long one.

She followed the trail back the way they had come in; on guard and fully aware that, somewhere out here, Tim's bitch sister and faceless brother were lurking.

During her trek, she fully expected them to show up, to ruin her escape, but that didn't happen. Perhaps they had scuttled off somewhere to try and recover from their wounds, or had taken a different route back to the house. If so, she hoped they found nothing but a blazing inferno and were helpless to do anything other than watch their home burn.

As Ashley walked, a new morning finally broke through the darkness. Shortly after, she finally passed out of the woods and into the open fields.

Back to the wilderness.

Once free of those cursed woods, she kept going for over an hour straight, making sure she put plenty of distance behind her.

Then she finally stopped, collapsed to the floor, and wept.

It was as if a switch had been flipped. Every feeling of sadness and loss and anger that had been pushed beneath the surface finally got release and erupted from her in a wave.

She cried and cried, loudly and desperately.

She remembered Kim and Craig, and what had become of them. She remembered the pain and terror she had endured.

She remembered it all.

But it would not ruin her, it would not define her.

She wouldn't let it.

Dealing with what had happened would take time and a lot of tears.

But she would deal with it all.

Ashley gave herself a few more moments, then got back to her feet, holding the book close to her. From the small snippets she had seen within it, she was certain it would read like the ramblings of a madman.

The thing was, she knew it was true. All of it. Hopefully, the book would explain the things she'd faced out here and help her to come to terms with what had happened.

Then again, maybe knowing the truth behind all of this wasn't something she needed in her life.

But she could make that decision herself, in time.

Ashley dug her hand into her pocket, felt the cold metal of Kim's lighter, safe with her, and pressed on.

She had no idea how she would explain things, or what lay ahead for her.

There was still a hell trek to overcome before she reached anything approaching civilisation, and she had no supplies other than the clothes on her back.

No food, no water, no shelter.

Nothing.

After everything she'd been through, Ashley realised something as simple as Mother Nature could actually be the death of her.

But she wouldn't allow that to happen.

She wasn't the same person as the one who had walked into those woods the day before.

She would make it, and she would survive.

Of that, Ashley had no doubt.

THE END

TORMENTED

Tormented

WELCOME TO ARLINGTON ASYLUM, A PLACE WHERE THE INSANE AND THE FORGOTTEN ARE BROUGHT TO DIE .

Adrian James is running from his past with nothing left to live for. At rock bottom, with a blade to his wrist, a mysterious stranger intervenes and offers him a chance at salvation.

Adrian accepts, and he enters Arlington Asylum of his own free will. Once inside, however, he soon learns that he will never escape. And worse, there are strange experiments taking place here, and a secretive medicine is being administered, one that causes certain... changes... in the patients.

The insidious secrets within the halls of Arlington

Asylum are slowly revealed, and it is beyond anything Adrian could have possibly imagined. A literal hell is unleashed as impossible and terrifying creatures indulge their sadistic desires.

Adrian and his friends must escape this nightmarish place and warn the outside world before it's too late, but they must face down the demons of hell to do so.

TORMENTED is a gruesome and violent horror story, influenced by such greats as John Carpenter's THE THING, Clive Barker's HELLRAISER, and Jeremy Gillespie's THE VOID.

Do you dare enter the Asylum?

THE DEMONIC

The Demonic

Years ago Danni Morgan ran away from her childhood home and vowed never to go back. It was a place of fear, pain and misery at the hands of an abusive father.

But now Danni's father is dead and she is forced to break her vow and return home—to lay his body to rest and face up to the ghosts of her past.

But Danni is about to realise that some ghosts are more real than others. And something beyond her understanding is waiting for her there, lurking in the shadows. An evil that intends to kill her family and claim her very soul.

Experience supernatural horror in the vein of THE CONJURING, INSIDIOUS and the legendary GHOST-

WATCH. THE DEMONIC will get under your skin, send chills down your spine and have you sleeping with the lights on!

THE MARK

The Mark

A SATANIC CULT. A WOMAN'S BRUTAL ASSAULT. CAN SHE FACE HER DARKEST FEAR BEFORE A DEMON IS UNLEASHED FROM HELL?

Kirsty Thompson is no stranger to trauma. But when a vicious attack leaves her drugged and disoriented, she never expected to wake up to a permanent scar. She starts having demonic visions, all linked to the ancient symbol carved deep into her back...

With the help of her best friend Amanda, Kirsty discovers that the mark originates from The Devil's Bible and forges a connection between her and a terrifying creature. As they track the man who assaulted her to a satanic cult, the beast hunts them from the shadows. Can Kirsty escape the devil worshippers and her bond with the heinous creature to save herself from eternal damnation?

The Mark is a terrifying standalone horror novel. If you like mysterious depraved forces, tales of the occult, and stories that will have you looking under the bed, then you'll love this gripping tale!

THE HOBBES HALL DIARIES

Sign up to my mailing list for The Hobbes Hall Diaries...

Liked Horror in the Woods? It was just the start.

A seemingly unrelated event took place in 2014. This diary is proof of that.

But is there more to all of this than we realise? Sinister beings exist in a place beyond our understanding. And worse—they have turned their attention to us...

Simply go to my website (www.leemountford.com) and sign up to my mailing list to get your free stories.

ABOUT THE AUTHOR

Lee Mountford was born and raised in the North East of England, in the small town of Ferryhill. Not much happens there, but it has a surprisingly dark history (seriously, just Google the Brass Farm Murders!).

He is an emerging author with a huge passion for horror, and Horror in the Woods is his first novel.

He still lives in the North East of England, with his amazing wife, Michelle. They are currently expecting their first child.

For more information
www.leemountford.com
leemountford01@googlemail.com

ACKNOWLEDGMENTS

Thanks first and foremost to my editor, Josiah Davis (http://www.jdbookservices.com), for such an amazing job. If anything is wrong with this book, that's on me. If anything is good with it, I'll only take half credit! The rest is down to him.

I'd also like to thank Dave Kawamoto, who kindly offered his services as a Beta-Reader. He offered up some fantastic suggestions that greatly helped the book.

The cover, which I'm thrilled with, was supplied by Debbie at The Cover Collection (http://www.thecovercollection.com).

Thanks as well to fellow author, and guru extraordinaire, Iain Rob Wright, for all of his fantastic advice and guidance. If you don't know who Iain is, remedy that now: http://www.iainrobwright.com

And the last thank you is the most important—to my amazing wife, Michelle, and daughter, Ella. You are both my world. Thank you for everything.

ISBN-13:

978-1974287734

ISBN-10:

1974287734

Created with Vellum

Made in the USA
Columbia, SC
21 June 2020